721 SECRETS

Keeping you up to date on all that goes on at Manhattan's most elite address!

The hottest ticket in town—or at least at 721 Park Avenue—is the 5th anniversary party of Reed and Elizabeth Wellington. At Manhattan's top hotel, it's the place to see and be seen. And apparently, there's *lots* to see with the Wellingtons. Rumor has it that Elizabeth's been trying hard to conceive—though one wonders how hard it could be when your husband is a blue-eyed babe like Reed. Maybe that's why he whisked her away to the French Riviera for a whirlwind vacation. Doting Reed has also hired his wife a chauffeur. Though some suspect the burly driver's really a bodyguard. For a hopeful mother-to-be? Either way, there have been so many comings and goings up in Penthouse A, so many whisperings, that you can't help wondering what else Reed is up to. Here's some advice: Baby-making takes two, so get busy, Reed. Meanwhile, we'll polish the silver spoon!

Dear Reader,

In 2006, I took my first trip to New York City. I'd expected the crowds, the skyscrapers, the traffic and the noise. What I hadn't expected was the sheer beauty and magnificence of Manhattan. We toured the Met, climbed to the top of the Empire State Building and strolled through Central Park. The restaurants and clubs were amazing, and everywhere we went, we found the best of the best. By the end of the trip, I realized if a person was going to be rich, they ought to be so in New York.

Enter Reed Wellington, my über-wealthy hero of *Marriage, Manhattan Style*. What better place for his penthouse than 721 Park Avenue, amidst the finest the city has to offer? He should be leading an exceedingly enjoyable life. And he is—until he receives a blackmail letter, is named in a Securities Exchange Commission investigation and is threatened with a divorce. He quickly realizes it'll take more than wealth and power to fight his way out of the legal mess and win back his wife, Elizabeth.

I hope you enjoy the story!

Barbara

MARRIAGE, MANHATTAN STYLE

BARBARA DUNLOP

Published by Silhouette Books
America's Publisher of Contemporary Romance

For the Berry Street and Schoolhouse Girls.
Sorry I missed the reunion!
Special thanks and acknowledgment to Barbara Dunlop for her contribution to the PARK AVENUE SCANDALS miniseries.

 SILHOUETTE BOOKS

ISBN-13: 978-0-373-76897-4
ISBN-10: 0-373-76897-4

MARRIAGE, MANHATTAN STYLE

Visit Silhouette Books at www.eHarlequin.com

Printed in U.S.A.

Books by Barbara Dunlop

Silhouette Desire

Thunderbolt over Texas #1704
Marriage Terms #1741
The Billionaire's Bidding #1793
The Billionaire Who Bought Christmas #1836
Beauty and the Billionaire #1853
Marriage, Manhattan Style #1897

BARBARA DUNLOP

writes romantic stories while curled up in a log cabin in Canada's far north, where bears outnumber people, and it snows six months of the year. Fortunately, she has a brawny husband and two teenage children to haul firewood and clear the driveway while she sips cocoa and muses about her upcoming chapters. Barbara loves to hear from readers. You can contact her through her Web site at www.barbaradunlop.com.

Who's Who at 721 Park Avenue

6A: Marie Endicott—The investigation continues into her mysterious demise…could someone in the building be responsible?

9B: Amanda Crawford—The cheerful event planner has been acting quite strange lately… does it have anything to do with her new client?

9B: Julia Prentice—The society girl has married infamous Wall Street millionaire Max Rolland… and there's a baby on the way.

12A: Vivian Vannick-Smythe—The building's longest-standing resident, who has been on edge lately. Could it be planning the celebration of the building's landmark status, or something else?

12B: Prince Sebastian of Caspia—The infamous royal has announced his upcoming nuptials to his longtime assistant, Tessa Banks!

12C: Trent Tanford—The building's playboy will be taking the plunge with Carrie Gray any day now.

Penthouse A: Reed and Elizabeth Wellington—Will the secrets surrounding this supposedly happy union emerge?

Penthouse B: Gage Lattimer—It seems the shadowy billionaire has his eyes set on a very unsuspecting female.

One

Elizabeth Wellington flicked the liberty head, ten-dollar gold coin high into the air above her king-size bed.

"Heads," she whispered to herself in the empty bedroom, her gaze following the coin's twirling trajectory toward the pale, bamboo ceiling mural, "I do it."

If it was tails, she'd wait until next week. At the proper time. When she was ovulating, and her chances of conceiving were at their best.

"Come on, heads," she muttered, picturing her husband, Reed, next door in his home office, studying e-mails or reading a financial report, looking fit and sexy and aloof, his mind firmly locked on the business of the day.

The coin nicked the far edge of the down comforter before bouncing onto the tightly woven carpet.

"Damn." She rounded the four-poster, blinking in vain at the dark burgundy pattern, trying to make out the shiny disk.

After a minute, she kicked off her shoes, dropped to her knees and hiked up her straight, charcoal skirt. Leaning on the heels of her hands, she peered under the bed. Was it heads or tails? And where the heck was the twenty-five thousand dollar collector coin?

"Elizabeth?" came Reed's voice from the hallway.

Guiltily, she jumped up, dusting off and straightening her hair.

"Yes?" she called back, catching a glimpse of the open, satin-lined, rosewood coin collection box. She scooted to the chest of drawers and shut the lid.

The bedroom door opened, and she struck what she hoped was a casual pose.

"Have you seen my PDA?" he asked.

"Uh, no." She moved away from the dresser and spotted the coin. It was tipped up against the nightstand, winking under the glow from the Tiffany lamp.

Reed glanced around the room. "I could have sworn I put it in my pocket before I left the office."

"Did you call it?" she asked, easing toward the coin, planning to camouflage it with her bare foot before his roving gaze landed on it.

She sure didn't want to have to explain this one.

"Can you dial it for me?" he asked.

"Sure." She lifted the bedside phone and punched in his cell number, putting herself between Reed and the coin, careful not to disturb its resting place and ruin the toss.

A tone trilled from somewhere in the penthouse.

"Thanks," he told her, turning for the door.

A few seconds later, he called "Got it" from the living room.

Elizabeth breathed a sigh of relief.

She eased her foot away and checked out the coin's position. It was supported by the wood molding, just a hair off vertical. She upped the light on the three-way bulb and leaned her head down. If the nightstand hadn't got in the way, and the momentum had kept it going, it would have been… Yes! Heads.

She snatched up the coin. The decision was made. She was taking her best friend's advice over that of a trained medical professional.

On the surface, her decision flew in the face of common sense. But her friend Hanna knew more about her life than Dr. Wendell.

Oh, the good doctor knew all about Elizabeth's physical health. He knew her hormone levels and her menstrual cycle. He'd even seen an ultrasound of her ovaries. But he didn't know about her marriage. He didn't know that she'd been fighting since her first anniversary to get back to the honesty and intimacy she and Reed had shared in the beginning.

In the five years since she'd married Reed Wellington III, Elizabeth had learned that the corporation came first, the New York business community second, the extended Wellington family third, with their own marriage somewhere further down the list.

She knew a baby would smooth things out. They'd both wanted one for years. A baby would give them a focal point, something to share, a way for her to fit more neatly into his world, and a reason for him to spend more time in hers. She'd been counting on a baby for a long time. But it was getting harder to convince herself that a baby alone was the answer.

A baby needed a warm and loving home. Children needed to experience intimacy, emotion and authenticity. The further she and Reed drifted apart, the closer Elizabeth came to admitting that even their dream of starting a family wouldn't set things right.

She carefully placed the coin back in the rosewood box, closing the lid and smoothing her fingertips over the whorls and scrolls that decorated the top. Reed had given her the liberty head coin and the rosewood box their first Christmas together. Then he'd added new coins every year. But, as the value of the collection grew, the strength of their marriage declined.

Ironic, really. Back when she had only one coin, they'd joked together, shared secrets, made mistakes and laughed together. More often than not ending up on the bed or the couch or the carpet if no soft furniture was immediately handy.

The first time they'd made love, it was on the padded bench of a gazebo in the massive backyard of his family's Connecticut estate. The dark, clear sky was dotted with stars. They were alone together, and Reed's kisses had turned passionate, his hands roaming the edges of the deep back of her cocktail dress. She'd felt her skin tingle, her nipples tighten and throbbing desire pool in the pit of her stomach.

The time for waiting had passed. They both knew it, and he'd pulled her down on the bench. After long minutes, maybe hours of kisses and caresses, he'd dispatched her panties. Then he buried himself deep inside her. Two weeks later, he'd proposed, and she had enthusiastically talked herself into happily ever after.

Her friends and family in New Hampshire had warned her against marrying a billionaire. His old family money put him in a completely different social class. And they'd told her that her and Reed's expectations of marriage might be completely different. But Elizabeth had been certain their deep love would conquer all obstacles.

Now, five years later, and a whole lot less certain, she moved to the glass balcony doors of her opulent bedroom. Below her penthouse on the twelfth floor of 721 Park Avenue, traffic hummed, and the lights of the cityscape rolled off toward the horizon on this mild, October night. She tugged the heavy curtains closed.

Although she'd recognized the wisdom in Hanna's advice, Elizabeth had felt better putting the decision in the hands of fate. The toss was heads, so the choice was made. She was fighting for her marriage in a different way, starting this minute.

She marched back to the cherrywood chest. The pewter handle was cool under her fingertips as she slid the top drawer open. She thumbed her way through dainty nightgowns and peignoirs, making her way to the bottom of the stack.

And there it was.

Her stomach fluttered as she slid out the red silk negligee she'd worn on her wedding night.

She unzipped the back of her skirt, shimmying out,

tossing her jacket, blouse and underwear on a chair, suddenly anxious to get to Reed. She slipped into the negligee, feeling decadently beautiful for the first time in months. Then she crossed to the en suite, fluffing her auburn hair.

Her eyelashes were dark and thick against her green eyes, her pupils slightly dilated. She freshened her lipstick, stroked some blush over her cheeks, then stepped back to check out the effect in the full-length mirror. Her feet were bare, toenails polished a gleaming copper, and the red silk fell mere inches down her thighs, ending in a band of sheer lace. The neckline dipped low, with more lace that barely camouflaged her breasts.

As a final touch, she dabbed some perfume on her neck and dropped one of the spaghetti straps off her shoulder. Then she stretched to her full five foot five and placed a hand over her fluttering abdomen. Her three-carat diamond winked back at her in the mirror.

Reed was her husband, she reminded herself. She had every right to seduce him. Besides, Hanna would be proud.

She headed across the bedroom, switching off the lamp and padding down the hallway.

"Reed?" she cooed softly, emerging into the doorway of his office, snaking her arm up the cool doorjamb and striking a pose.

Two men looked up from where they were reading a letter.

At the sight of his wife's sexy outfit, Reed's jaw fell open, the words *insider trading* vanishing from his mind. The Securities and Exchange Commission's letter slipped from his fingers to the desktop while, beside him, his vice president, Collin Killian, sucked in a shocked breath.

It took Collin a full three seconds to think to turn away. Reed supposed he couldn't blame the man. It took Elizabeth five seconds to squeak out a gasp and flee down the hall.

"Uh…" Collin began, peering cautiously over his shoulder at the now empty doorway.

Reed swore as he rose to his feet and heard the bedroom door slam shut.

Collin reached for his briefcase. "Catch you later."

"You stay put," Reed commanded, striding across the room.

"But—"

"I just found out I'm being investigated by the SEC. You and I need to talk."

"But your wife—"

"I'll talk to her first." What was Elizabeth thinking? He rounded the corner into the hall.

Collin called behind him, "I don't think talking is what she has in mind."

Reed didn't bother answering.

Elizabeth had no business doing anything *but* talking. He wasn't the one monitoring her basal body temperature, but he was pretty sure they were days ahead of schedule. He missed spontaneous lovemaking as much as she must, but he also wanted to be a father. And he knew damn well she wanted to be a mother. Programmed lovemaking was frustrating. But it was a sacrifice worth making.

He put his hand on the doorknob, forcing himself to pause, steeling his hormones for the sight he knew waited inside. His wife was a knockout, a sexy, sensual, stunning knockout, but he had to be strong for both of them.

He turned the knob and carefully opened the door.

"Elizabeth?"

"Go away." Her voice was muffled as she wrapped a terry robe protectively around herself. A stream of light from the en suite backlit her as he shut the door and moved into the room.

"What's going on?" he asked softly.

She shook her head. "Nothing."

He longed to draw her into his arms, maybe slip his hands into the soft terry cloth and pull her tight against his body. It would take so little to nudge the robe open, reveal the negligee beneath, and to gaze on her luscious body. Collin would figure out that he should leave.

"Is it the right time?" Reed asked instead, knowing it wasn't possible that she was ovulating, but still hoping against hope.

She slowly shook her head.

He allowed himself to move a step closer. "Then what are you doing?"

"I thought…" She paused. "I wanted…" Her green eyes blinked up at him. "I didn't know Collin was here."

Reed almost twitched a smile. "No kidding."

Her hand went to her forehead. "He must think—"

"At the moment, he thinks I'm the luckiest man in the world."

She fixed him with a probing gaze. "But you're not."

"Not tonight."

Her gaze slid away.

"Elizabeth?"

She looked back. "I thought… We aren't…"

He was pretty sure he knew where she was going. It was tempting, damn tempting. At this moment, he wanted nothing more than to make passionate love on their big, four-poster bed and pretend none of their problems existed.

He was willing to put off talking about the SEC investigation. But he wasn't willing to compromise on their family. If they made love now, Elizabeth wouldn't get pregnant again this month, and her tears would break Reed's heart.

"Can you hold that thought until next week?" he asked.

Hurt and disappointment clouded her eyes. She opened her mouth to speak, but then she clenched her teeth, compressing her lips and squeezing her eyes shut for a couple of seconds.

When she opened them, her expression had smoothed out, and she seemed under control again. "Is there something going on? Why is Collin—"

"Nothing's going on," Reed quickly assured her.

Nothing but what had to be a completely bogus investigation, which Collin would quash as soon as humanly possible.

Reed hadn't engaged in insider trading, or any other illegal or unethical business practice for that matter. Still, he couldn't help speculating on the maximum sentence. In the current climate for white-collar crime, he imagined they'd try to throw the book at him.

That's why they had to make this go away, and fast.

It had to go away before the press or anybody else got wind of it. Including Elizabeth. Especially Elizabeth.

Their specialist said infertility was often related to stress, and she was stressed enough about trying to get pregnant, not to mention planning their fifth anniversary party. The last thing she needed was to worry about a potential court case.

"I have to head down to Collin's apartment for a little while," he told her.

Her voice went flat, the disbelief evident. "A little while?"

"It's a routine matter," said Reed, vowing to wrap the discussion up quickly.

She nodded. "Of course."

"Why don't you work on the catering menu while I'm gone?" Three hundred guests were invited to the up-coming party; there had to be a million details that required her attention.

"Sure," she said, without enthusiasm. "I'll study the dessert menu for a while."

The sarcastic remark was unlike Elizabeth, and Reed knew he should ask her what was wrong. But he was afraid to get into it, afraid it might lead him to embrace her, to kiss her, to throw all of his good intentions out the window. There was only so much temptation a man could take.

"I'll see you in an hour," he said huskily instead, allowing himself one quick, chaste kiss on her forehead.

His hand brushed her hair, sending tingles of desire all the way up to his shoulder. Her fingers closed over his wrist for the briefest of moments. It was enough to make him question his decision to leave.

But he had to walk out. He'd promised himself he'd do everything in his power to give her a baby. And he would.

Without meeting her eyes, he turned for the door, marched down the hall to where Collin hovered beside the desk, a decidedly uncertain expression on his face.

"Let's go," said Reed, slipping into his suit jacket and leading the way to the penthouse door.

Collin didn't ask any questions. Discretion was one of the things Reed liked best about the man.

"I've got the SEC letter," Collin confirmed as the door closed behind them, and they headed for Gage Lattimer's penthouse. Collin's friend, Gage, had also been named in the SEC's letter as being part of the investigation.

"Envelope, too?" asked Reed. He didn't want a shred of evidence lying around for Elizabeth to stumble across.

"Everything," said Collin, stopping in front of the wide oak door. "And I closed your Web browser."

"Thanks." Reed nodded, giving a sharp knock.

They waited in silence, listening to a clang and clash from inside. The door was finally opened. But it wasn't Gage standing in front of them. It was a tall, attractive brunette with a guarded, almost guilty look in her green eyes.

"Is Gage available?" asked Reed, hoping he wasn't disturbing something. Although the woman *was* fully dressed.

"I'm terribly sorry—" The woman cleared her throat. "Mr. Lattimer isn't in at the moment."

Was that a British accent?

"And you are?" asked Collin.

"Jane Elliott. Mr. Lattimer's new housekeeper."

Reed's gaze caught on the untidy penthouse over her shoulder.

She pulled the door against her back, blocking his view. "May I tell him who called?"

"Reed Wellington."

Collin handed the woman a business card. "Can you ask him to call me as soon as possible?"

"Of course," she replied with a nod, then slipped back into the suite and closed the door.

"I hope he's not paying her much," Reed mused as they turned for the elevator.

"I'd pay her pretty much anything she asked," said Collin.

Reed couldn't help but smile as he punched the call button for the elevator. Then he quickly brought his thoughts back to the problem at hand. "So what in the hell do you think is going on with this?" Reed asked as the doors slid open to an empty car.

"I think maybe you should have paid the blackmail."

Reed drew back. As a wealthy man, he was often the target of both financial appeals and threats. But a particularly bizarre blackmail demand had arrived two weeks ago.

"Ten million dollars?" he asked Collin. "Are you out of your mind?"

"The two could be related."

"The blackmail letter said, 'the world will learn the dirty secret of how the Wellingtons make their money.' It didn't say anything about an SEC investigation." Not that Reed would have paid up in any event. But he might have taken the letter a little more seriously if the threat had been that specific.

"Insider trading is a dirty little secret."

"It's also a ridiculous fabrication."

When Reed first read the blackmail letter, he'd dismissed it as a hoax. There were plenty of lunatics out there. Then he'd wondered if some of their overseas suppliers might be engaged in unethical labor practices. But he'd checked them all out. He could find absolutely nothing to substantiate any "dirty little secret" of the Wellingtons' wealth.

He had no dirty little secret. It was beyond preposterous to suggest he'd engaged in insider trading. And impossible to prove, since he hadn't done it. It wasn't even logical. The vast majority of his and his father's and, for that matter, their ancestors' wealth was derived from the performance of their companies. Reed did very little trading on the stock market.

And what little he did do was recreational, just to see if he could beat the odds. Where was the challenge in cheating? He didn't need the money. And cheating wouldn't be any fun. So why the hell would he engage in insider trading?

"They've got something," said Collin as the elevator came to a rest on the second floor. "The SEC doesn't start investigations on spec."

"So, who do we call?" asked Reed.

As well as being a vice president, Collin was a damn fine lawyer. He inserted his key and opened the apartment door. "The SEC for starters."

Reed glanced at his watch. Nine-fifteen. "You know anybody we can disturb?"

"Yeah." Collin tossed his briefcase on the table of the more compact, one-bedroom apartment that was owned by Wellington International. "I know a guy." He picked up a cordless phone. "You feel like pouring the scotch?"

"On it."

Collin's call was brief.

When he finished, he accepted a crystal tumbler of single malt and sat back in an armchair. "They'll send us a full dossier in the morning, but it's something to do with Ellias Technologies."

Reed recognized the company name. "That was Gage's deal. He thought they were going to go big, so we both bought in." But he couldn't believe Gage Lattimer, his friend and neighbor, would have recommended a stock based on insider information. But he went over the scenario, thinking out loud as he stepped through the deal.

"It did shoot up fast. Particularly when that navigations system—"

A lightbulb went on inside Reed's head.

"What?" Collin prompted.

"Kendrick."

"The senator?"

Reed nodded. "Damn it. How much you want to bet he was on the approval committee?"

The trepidation in Collin's voice was obvious. "Not the one that awarded the navigations contract."

"Yeah." Reed took a swallow of his scotch. "That one."

Collin cursed under his breath.

Reed echoed the sentiment. He hadn't done anything wrong, but if Kendrick was on the approval committee, it would sure look like he had.

"I buy shares in Ellias," Reed speculated out loud. "Kendrick—who the whole world *knows* is an avid supporter of my Envirocore.com—approves a lucrative contract for Ellias. Ellias stock soars. I make a few hundred thousand. And suddenly the SEC is involved."

"You missed a step," said Collin.

"The blackmailer," Reed agreed. If the blackmailer was the one who alerted the SEC, then Reed hadn't taken him nearly seriously enough.

The blackmailer obviously had information on Reed's stock portfolio. He also knew Reed was the owner of Envirocore. And he knew that Kendrick was on the Senate navigation system contract approval committee. What's more, he knew how to put it all together to hurt Reed.

This was no lightweight.

Collin gazed at the storm-tossed seascape on his far wall. "Nobody in his right mind is going to think you broke the law for a few hundred thousand."

"Are you kidding? Everybody's ready to knock old money off their pedestal."

"Can you prove you're innocent?"

Reed scoffed. "Prove that a phone call, a meeting or an e-mail *didn't* take place? I don't see how I can do that."

"Did you call the police on the blackmail letter?"

"I filed it with the rest of the crank stuff." Mistake. Obviously.

"You want to call them tonight?"

Reed nodded. "We might as well get this party started."

Two

The black-tie hospital fund-raiser at the Bergere Grande Hotel was in full swing on Saturday night. Guests had been served a gourmet dinner in the Crystal Room, and now they were moving through the marble-pillared foyer to the East Ballroom for cocktails and dancing.

Elizabeth had spotted Collin approaching, so she'd quickly set a course for the ladies' room. She knew she'd have to look the man in the eye at some point, but she was putting off the moment as long as possible. She didn't want to think about how much the red negligee had revealed.

She emerged from checking her hair and freshening her lipstick and accepted a flute of champagne from a smartly dressed waiter. Then she concentrated on a series of silent auction items on her way to the main ballroom. She wanted to give Collin and Reed plenty of time to finish their conversation.

Hanna sidled up to her. "So, how'd it go last night?"

Elizabeth bought a little time by putting her head down over an auction item. It was a ruby and diamond choker, and the top bid was ten thousand dollars. She added a thousand and signed her name.

"Nice," said Hanna, nodding to the jewels that were secured in a glass case. "If you win, can I borrow it sometime?"

"Sure."

Hanna latched on to Elizabeth's arm and drew her away from the crowd. "So, did you do it?"

Elizabeth admitted as much with a nod.

"What happened?"

"I crashed and burned."

Hanna's sculpted brows knit together. "I don't understand. Was he asleep or something?"

"I got dressed up in a red, slinky negligee." Elizabeth omitted the part about the coin toss, not wanting Hanna to know she'd had second thoughts. "Then I surprised him in his office."

"And?" Hanna prompted, cocking her expertly coiffed blond hair to one side.

"And Collin was there, too."

Hanna's fingertips went to her mouth to cover her grin.

"Don't you dare laugh," Elizabeth warned in a dire undertone. "I was mortified."

"Were you…exposed?"

Elizabeth sniffed, attempting to regain her dignity. "There was no frontal nudity."

"He saw your butt?" Hanna looked somewhat thrilled at the prospect.

"He did not see my butt. It was a negligee. It was sexy, but it covered everything that counts."

"So, what's the problem?"

"I tried to vamp up my husband, and he left for a meeting with Collin." Elizabeth's gaze slid across the room to where the two men were talking. There were things more embarrassing than having Collin see her in her red negligee.

"Oh," said Hanna, obviously understanding the broader point.

"Yes. *Oh*. Apparently I'm not nearly as irresistible as I'd hoped."

Hanna's red mouth pursed in puzzlement. "What exactly did he say?"

Elizabeth's tone turned sharp, even though she knew none of this was Hanna's fault. "Do we have to dissect it?"

"Of course we have to dissect it. How else are we going to learn from it?"

"Fine." Elizabeth took a breath. Hanna wanted the gory details? "He said 'I have to go meet with Collin. I'll be back in an hour. You should work on the anniversary party catering menu.'" She was beginning to hate that catering menu. "He also said 'Hold that thought.'"

"Ouch," Hanna whispered in sympathy.

Elizabeth peered into the main ballroom. "Let's go find the bar."

"Yeah," Hanna agreed with a rush of breath.

"There are times in a woman's life when she absolutely needs a drink."

They started toward the main ballroom. Elizabeth wanted to hurry and disappear, but she was forced to move carefully in her sleek, silver evening gown.

"Vannick-Smythe at three o'clock," Hanna warned in an undertone.

Elizabeth's gaze flicked to her gossipy neighbor Vivian and made eye contact. "Uh-oh. She spotted us."

Hanna bent her head. "Pretend we're deep in conversation."

"Right."

"I'm surprised she didn't bring her dogs," said Hanna, referring to Vivian Vannick-Smythe's yappy white Shih Tzus. Constantly by her side, the two dogs went uncannily well with the woman's overdyed hair.

"I guess she couldn't get them on the guest list," Elizabeth speculated.

Hanna sputtered out a laugh. "Oops. Here she comes." Then she raised her voice to conversation level. "And what did you think of yesterday's political coup in Barasmundi?"

Elizabeth quickly jumped into the game. "I don't think a woman can hold on to power in West Africa." She resisted the urge to glance at Vivian, as the woman came to a halt beside them. "But if Maracitu can pull off the elections, it'll help stabilize the north, maybe inspire the tribal leaders to participate in democratic rule."

Hanna was a network news anchor, and an all-around political junkie. Elizabeth assumed her ploy was to make the conversation as inaccessible as possible for Vivian.

Luckily, Elizabeth was interested in world politics herself. It was one of the reasons she and Hanna had become such good friends.

Hanna put in, "I don't see how the government can move ahead on the constitutional vote if—"

"Well, I certainly didn't expect to see *you* here." Vivian Vannick-Smythe's drawl overrode Hanna's words.

Elizabeth glanced up to see Vivian's penetrating gaze fixed on her. The hostile tone took her by surprise. "Hello, Vivian."

Vivian sniffed. "At minimum, one would think you'd let the speculation die down."

"What speculation?" Had somebody heard she was trying to get pregnant? Or had Collin gossiped about her failed seduction attempt?

"Why, the SEC investigation, my dear," said Vivian, a flash of triumph in her eyes and a cruel smile fighting its way to life on her face. "I don't know what that husband of yours got up to. And, of course, it's none of *my* business, but when the SEC starts investigating—"

"Vivian Vandoosen, isn't it?" Hanna elbowed her way between the two women and stuck out her hand, giving Elizabeth's mind time to scramble for a foothold on logic.

Vivian's glare all but scalded Hanna. "Vannick-Smythe," she corrected in an imperious voice.

"Of course," said Hanna. "It must have slipped my mind. You understand how it is. I meet so many *important* people in my job, others sometimes get lost in the shuffle."

Any other time, Elizabeth would have laughed at the insulted expression on Vivian's face.

"I'm afraid you'll have to excuse us," said Hanna, linking her elbow through Elizabeth's, all but dragging her away from the stunned Vivian.

"What's she talking about?" Elizabeth hissed under her breath as they passed the fountain, heading toward the patio doors.

"I assumed you knew," said Hanna, making a beeline for the ballroom. "The story won't break until tomorrow."

Elizabeth stopped abruptly. "There's a story?"

Hanna looked uncomfortable. "Bert Ralston is working on it right now."

Elizabeth felt her eyes go wide at the mention of the network's top investigative reporter. "It's that big?"

Hanna nodded apologetically. "Your husband and Gage Lattimer are under investigation for insider trading in Ellias Technologies stock."

Elizabeth was speechless.

"Let's find a drink," said Hanna.

"How... I don't..." Insider trading? Reed would never do something dishonest.

"How do you not know?" asked Hanna, stopping in front of a bar and the uniformed bartender who stood behind a row of sparkling glasses and a garnish tray. "Two vodka martinis."

"He didn't tell me."

Hanna nodded while the man mixed the drinks. "Really."

"Why didn't he tell me?"

Hanna scooped up the drinks and held one out to Elizabeth as they walked away. "Can't help you there."

Elizabeth closed her fingers over the fine stem of the

glass. Her husband was a subject of a criminal investigation, and he hadn't bothered to mention it?

Last night he'd told her nothing was going on. That it was a routine matter. Though clearly Collin knew what was up.

Reed's employees knew more than his wife did. The network news knew more than she did. Even Vivian Vannick-Smythe knew more than she did.

How could Reed have put her in this position?

"Is my marriage already over?" asked Elizabeth, dread welling up inside her.

"I think," said Hanna, obviously choosing her words with care, "you're going to have to ask Reed that question."

Elizabeth took a gulp of the strong drink, determination replacing distress. "That's not the only question I'm going to ask him."

Elizabeth's green eyes glittered like emeralds as she turned on Reed in their penthouse foyer. "How do you not tell me you're under investigation by the SEC?"

Ah, there it was. She'd been uncharacteristically silent in the limo, so he'd known something was up. At least now he could mount a defense.

He flipped on an overhead light, latching the dead bolt behind them. "It's not a serious problem."

Her voice went up an octave. "Not a serious problem? They're handing out twenty-year jail sentences for white-collar crimes these days."

"I didn't do it," he pointed out.

She just smiled mulishly up at him.

"You've got me tried, convicted and jailed." Now, wasn't that a vote of confidence?

"I haven't convicted you. I'm frightened for you."

"You sound angry."

"I'm both."

"You don't need to be."

"Oh, well. Thanks. That makes it all better."

"You think sarcasm's the answer?" He was perfectly willing to talk about this. But he wanted to have a reasonable, rational discussion. Mostly, he wanted to dispel her fears that he might be sentenced to jail.

"I think communication is the answer," she responded tartly. "You know, the part where you talk to me about what's going on in your life. Your hopes, your fears, your aspirations, your *pending criminal charges*."

"How would telling you have helped?" Reed truly wanted to know.

"We could have shared the load."

"You have your own load."

"We're husband and wife, Reed."

"And husbands don't unburden themselves by worrying their wives."

"Sure they do. All the time."

"Well, this husband doesn't. You have enough to think about right now—"

"You mean like the catering menu?"

"Among other things. There was no point in both of us worrying, and I didn't want to upset you."

"Well, I'm plenty upset now."

"You should stop." He was going to take care of it.

It was only a matter of time before this was wrapped up and life got back on track.

"You're joking, right?"

"It's nothing." He stepped toward her. "It'll blow over in no time."

She tipped up her chin to look at him. "What did you do?"

"Nothing."

"I meant to make them suspicious."

"Nothing," he repeated with conviction.

"So, the SEC is conducting random investigations on innocent and unsuspecting citizens?"

Reed drew a heavy sigh. He really didn't have the energy to go into it tonight. It was late and, even though tomorrow was Sunday, he had a conference call first thing in the morning. He wanted to sleep. He wanted her to sleep, too.

She cocked her head to one side. "Ellias Technologies?"

"I bought some shares," he reluctantly allowed. "So did Gage. Their value rose dramatically, and it tripped an alarm bell somewhere. Collin will take care of it. Now, let's go to bed."

"That's all the information I get?"

"That's all the information you need."

"I want more."

"Why does this have to be a thing?" Why couldn't she trust him to take care of it? It was his problem, not hers. Her fretting wouldn't help the situation one bit.

"Reed," she warned, all but tapping her foot.

"Fine." He stripped off his suit jacket and loosened

his tie. "It turns out that Senator Kendrick was on a committee that awarded Ellias Technologies a lucrative government contract."

Her green eyes narrowed. "And they think the senator gave you a heads up."

"Exactly," said Reed. "Are you happy now?"

"No. I am *not* happy now."

He raised his palms in a gesture of defeat. "And *that's* why I didn't tell you. I want you to be happy. I don't want you to worry." Was that so hard for her to understand?

Her lips pursed in that mulish expression that he recognized so well. "I don't need you protecting me."

He moved closer, moderating his voice. "The doctor said you should stay calm."

"How can I stay calm when my husband is lying to me?"

He hadn't lied to her. He'd omitted a small amount of unnecessary information so that she wouldn't get stressed out for no reason. "You're being ridiculous," he pointed out.

She pulled back. "Is that what you think?"

He could see her warming up for a whole new argument. Well, he wasn't buying into that at one in the morning.

"What I think is that Collin is on the case," he stated with conviction. "By next week, it'll be a footnote in my life. And you have much more important things to think about right now."

"Like the catering menu?" she repeated.

"Exactly. And your basal body temperature." He attempted to lighten the mood. "And that little red negligee."

"I do have a brain, you know, Reed."

It was his turn to draw back. Where the hell had that come from? "Have I ever suggested you don't?"

"I can help you solve problems."

"I pay professionals to help me solve problems." That way, he and Elizabeth could lead a calm, uncluttered life.

"That's your answer?"

"That's my answer."

Elizabeth waited for him to say more, but he was happy to end on that note.

Reed was the last to arrive at the lunch meeting in the Wellington International boardroom. Gage, Collin, media mogul Trent Tanford and private investigator Selina Marin were already sitting around the polished table when he walked in.

"Did you get hold of Kendrick?" Gage asked without preamble.

Reed shook his head, shutting the door behind him before taking his place at the head of the oblong table. Fresh-brewed coffee had been placed on the sideboard, and a bank of windows overlooked the fall colors of the park many stories below. "His secretary says he's in meetings in Washington all week."

"He doesn't have a cell phone?" asked Collin.

"He can't be disturbed," Reed quoted, letting his expression tell the room the excuse rang hollow to him. He'd never had a problem getting hold of Kendrick before. In fact, it was usually Kendrick who called him.

"We need his denial," said Trent. "At least, we need

him to publicly deny having given you insider information. And I'd prefer to have it on videotape."

"You'll have it," said Reed, hoping it would be soon. It was in everyone's best interest—including the senator's—to have him on the record in this. In the absence of identifying the blackmailer, Kendrick's backing was their best chance of stopping the investigation in its tracks.

"Did you get anywhere with the police?" Reed asked Selina.

"I had a chat with Detective Arnold McGray." She slid a thick sheaf of paper across the table to Reed. "They've been surprisingly cooperative. Here's the list of blackmail victims in the building."

"The cops are at a dead end," Collin put in. "They're hoping the extra manpower will help."

"Person power," Selina put in.

"Sorry," said Collin with an edge of sarcasm. "I keep forgetting you're a girl."

"Shall I start wearing pink ruffles?"

Reed contemplated Selina's no-nonsense black blazer, white turtleneck, short cropped hair and minimal makeup. With those dark brows and that straight slant to her mouth, she'd look ridiculous in pink.

Reed sighed and picked up the letter, reading the names of Julia Prentice, who before her marriage to Max Rolland was blackmailed regarding her out-of-wedlock pregnancy, Trent Tanford for his relationship with murder victim Marie Endicott, and Prince Sebastian who'd also received a threatening letter.

In the prince's case, the letter writer didn't ask for

any money, and it was eventually proven to be his ex-girlfriend. So, the Prince Sebastian incident didn't seem to be related.

"Any connection between mine and the other two?" Reed asked Selina.

"Three different threats," she answered. "Three unrelated incidents. Three untraceable Grand Cayman bank accounts." Then she paused. "Same bank."

Reed allowed himself a small smile. So, the three *were* likely related. That gave them a whole lot more information to go on.

"I'll start looking for connections between the cases," said Selina.

"Any guess as to why mine was ten million and the others were only one?" asked Reed.

Selina gave a wry twist of her lips. "Neither of the others paid up. Maybe expenses were mounting."

"You bet your ass we didn't pay up," muttered Trent.

"You should be flattered," Gage directed his comment to Reed. "The guy obviously thinks you're solvent."

"Flattered isn't exactly how I'm feeling." He didn't need this crap in his life. His life was plenty complicated enough.

"What about Marie Endicott's murder?" Collin brought up the topic they'd avoided so far.

"I don't like speculating about that," said Trent.

Neither did Reed. But ignoring the possibility that the murder was tied up in the blackmail scheme wouldn't change the facts, and it wouldn't reduce the danger.

"The police aren't ready to call it a murder," said Selina. "But that missing security tape makes my hair stand on end. And I think we have to operate on the assumption that they're connected."

"That's a pretty big assumption," said Collin.

"Yeah? Well, I'm preparing for the worst-case scenario." Then she turned to Trent. "I wonder. Did the blackmailer commit murder to set you up? Or did he target you after learning of the murder?"

"My guess would be that he's opportunistic," said Trent. "After the murder, he set me up."

"Generally," said Selina, "there are two reasons for a murder. Passion or greed."

"The blackmailer is definitely greedy," said Reed. "And if he operated on passion, we'd probably have another dead body, not more blackmail letters. He's got to be ticked off at us."

"Fair point," Collin put in.

"But we don't know anything for sure," said Trent.

Trent was right. And Reed wasn't in a position to take any chances. Three people in his building had been blackmailed and one was dead.

He slid the list back to Selina. "Hire as many people as you need. And put somebody on Elizabeth." Then he paused and drew a breath. "But tell him to keep his distance. Nobody talks to my wife about the blackmail." He glanced around the room to drive home his point.

Everybody nodded, and he rose to his feet.

He was keeping Elizabeth safe, but it was also his job to keep her calm. When this was over, they had a family to start. And, God help him, it was going to be over soon.

Three

"Your marriage is far from over," said Hanna as she and Elizabeth made their way past groups of diners to a corner table in their favorite deli off Times Square.

Out of habit, Elizabeth had ordered a thick corned beef on rye, but she was pretty sure her clenched stomach wouldn't allow her to eat.

"He won't talk to me about anything important," she told Hanna. "He won't make love with me. And when I ask for more information, he gets angry. How can I stay married to a man who won't let me into his life?"

Hanna took a sip of her diet cola. "Stop trying."

The answer set Elizabeth back in her chair. "Stop trying to be married?" That wasn't the answer she'd expected.

"Stop trying to muscle your way into his life." Hanna took a bite of her sandwich.

"That doesn't make any sense." They were married. Elizabeth was supposed to be in Reed's life.

Hanna peeled a paper napkin from the metal dispenser and dabbed the corners of her mouth. "I say this as your best friend, and as someone who loves you dearly—"

"This can't be good," Elizabeth mumbled.

"You've grown a little, well, dull lately."

Dull? What the heck kind of a thing was that for a good friend to say?

"You are *way* too invested in Reed and Reed's life."

"He's my husband."

Hanna shook her head. "Doesn't matter. I know you want a baby. And that's admirable. And I know you love Reed. And that's admirable, too. But, Elizabeth, Lizzy, you have got to get a life."

"I have a life."

Hanna gave her a dubious look.

Okay, so maybe working out at the spa, buying designer clothes and planning parties wasn't the most productive life. But Reed did a lot of corporate entertaining. It was important for her to look the part.

"If you had your own life," Hanna continued, "you wouldn't obsess so much about Reed's."

"I don't care what kind of a full, exciting and enriching life I'm leading, I'm still going to care that my husband is under criminal investigation."

"He told you he'd take care of it."

"Of course he told me that. He doesn't want me to worry. He's psychotic that way."

"I think it's sweet."

"*Sweet?* Whose side are you on?"

"Lizzy, you've lost all perspective. It's not about sides. It's about your happiness. Thing is, Reed's life centers around his job, his business associates, his family and friends, and his marriage."

"Not so much his marriage," Elizabeth muttered.

"Maybe. But that's not my point. My point is that your life also centers around *his* job, *his* business associates, *his* family and friends, and your marriage. See the problem?"

"That's not true." It couldn't be true. Elizabeth wasn't some 1950s throwback without a thought of her own.

"Who are your friends? Your old friends? The ones that have nothing to do with Reed?"

Elizabeth searched her brain, conjuring then discounting those people she'd grown up with or met at college.

"My old friends don't live in Manhattan," she finally answered.

After her marriage, it had quickly become difficult to spend time with her old friends. They seemed to think Elizabeth's life was one long party, that money solved everything, that rich people should never have a single problem. And, if they did, they should shut up about it and go shopping.

"And all of his do," said Hanna with an expression of triumph.

Elizabeth eyed her corned beef and decided she could use some comfort food after all. "Your point?"

"All of your current friends are really Reed's friends."

"Except for you."

"You met me through Trent. You remember Trent? Reed's friend."

"This is starting to feel like an intervention."

"That's because it is an intervention," said Hanna.

"Well, I don't need one."

Hanna let out a breath. "Oh, my darling…"

Elizabeth lifted the succulent sandwich. "I don't know why I should take your advice anyway. You were the one who insisted I seduce him last week. And that sure went to hell in a handbasket."

"That's because you did it wrong."

"I did it perfectly. I rocked in that red negligee. Reed was the problem. He was about to be arrested. How can a man concentrate on passion when he's about to be arrested?" Point well made, Elizabeth took a bite of her sandwich.

"You need a job," said Hanna.

Elizabeth swallowed. "Trust me on this. The one thing I don't need is more money."

Hanna waved her pickle. "It's not the paycheck. It's the getting out of the penthouse, exchanging opinions and ideas with other adults, hanging out with people who have absolutely nothing to do with your husband or with getting pregnant."

"And you don't think that will drag us further apart?"

"It'll give you something interesting to talk about when you get home."

Elizabeth was about to protest that they already talked about interesting things, but she stopped herself when she realized how hollow that would ring.

Reed was pretty much a workaholic, and he refused to discuss Wellington International with her. He seemed to think business problems would stress her out as much as SEC investigations. But if she introduced her own business issues, especially if there were problems, she was willing to bet he'd engage in the conversation.

Hmm. Getting a job. Developing an identity. The idea kind of appealed to her. In fact, she wondered why she hadn't thought of it before.

But there was a glitch. A big glitch.

"Who's going to hire me? I haven't worked since I graduated from college." She paused. "With a degree in musical theater."

"We're less than five blocks from the theater district," Hanna offered.

Elizabeth couldn't picture herself as a script girl or a gofer. It would be silly for the wife of a billionaire to take an entry-level position. Not to mention embarrassing for Reed.

"He doesn't have to like it," said Hanna, guessing the direction of Elizabeth's thoughts.

"Wouldn't that pretty much defeat the purpose?" She was trying to save her marriage not alienate her husband.

"What do *you* want?"

Elizabeth suddenly felt tired. "Raspberry cheesecake."

"And after that?"

"A baby. My marriage. To be happy. I don't know."

"Bingo," said Hanna.

"Bingo what?"

"Get happy. Get *yourself* happy. Independent of Reed or a baby or anything else. Make your own life work. The rest will have to sort itself out around that." Hanna paused, her blue eyes going soft along with her voice. "What have you got to lose?"

It was an excellent question. There was little left to lose. If something didn't change drastically and soon, she wouldn't have a marriage. She certainly wouldn't have a baby. She wouldn't have a life of any kind.

Hanna was right. She had to get out there and get a job.

A *job?*

Through the open door of the en suite, Reed watched Elizabeth rub scented lotion onto the smooth skin of one of her calves as she got ready for bed.

"You mean you want to sit on a charity board?" he asked. There were any number of worthy organizations that would be happy to have her support.

"Not a seat on a board," she answered. "I mean a real job."

Reed was stymied. "Why?"

She shrugged, putting the cap back on the bottle. "It'll get me out of the house, into the community, help me meet new people."

"You can get out of the house anytime you want."

This was New York, and she had an unlimited budget. There was no end to the things she could get out of the house and do, and no end to the people she could meet while doing them.

"Shopping doesn't give me the same sense of satisfaction."

He searched her expression, trying to figure out what was really going on. "There's more to life than shopping."

"Exactly." She stood up, replaced the bottle and selected a small jar of cream.

"The Hospital Foundation would be thrilled to have you on board."

"My degree is in theater."

"Then the Arts Board. I can make a call to Ralph Sitman. I'm sure one of the committees—"

"Reed, I don't want you to make a call. I want to type up my résumé and get out there and apply for a job."

"Your résumé?" he asked with disbelief. She was a Wellington. She didn't need a résumé.

"Yes." She turned to the mirror and rubbed the cream onto her forehead.

"You're planning to schlep around the theater district with a copy of the classifieds under your arm?"

"That's how it's generally done."

His voice went dark. "Not in this family, it isn't." If he was lucky, people would think she was eccentric. But some might actually think she needed the money. Like he was some miser who wouldn't see to her needs.

Elizabeth stepped back into the room, her diaphanous gown backlit until she shut off the en suite light. "Excuse me?"

"It's undignified," he told her.

"Earning a living is undignified?"

He tried to stay calm, but he could feel the tension mounting behind his eyes. "You already earn a living."

"No, you earn a living."

"And it's a damn good one."

She stepped forward and flipped back the comforter on her side of the bed. "Congratulations. Bully for you."

"Elizabeth," he pleaded. "What is going on?"

She folded her arms across her chest, unconsciously

thrusting her breasts out against the thin fabric. "I need a life, Reed."

What the hell kind of a statement was that? "You have a life."

"*You* have a life."

"It's *our* life."

"And you're never in it."

"I haven't left New York in months." And don't think that wasn't tough to orchestrate. But he wanted to be on deck for making babies, and he wanted to be around Elizabeth in case she needed anything. It was a tough time for both of them. He recognized that, and he was doing his best to keep things calm and smooth.

"You think this is about your physical presence in the city?"

"What is it about?" He paused. "Please, Elizabeth, for God's sake, tell me what this is all about."

She hesitated, her hands dropping back to her sides. "This is about me wanting a job."

"Doing what?"

"I don't know. Whatever I can get. Script girl, production assistant, gofer." She drew a breath and squared her shoulders. "This isn't negotiable, Reed."

He flipped back his side of the comforter, losing his grip on his temper, feeling the argument slip out of control.

"Great," he intoned. "Our friends and associates will show up to an opening at the Met. They'll all have dates. I'll be stag, because my wife will be the gofer."

"No. Elizabeth Wellington will be the gopher."

"And you don't think that'll be just a little humiliating for me?"

Her jaw clenched. "Then I'll use my maiden name."

"You'll use your real name," he growled.

"Fine." She flounced into bed, tugging the covers up to her chest.

Reed dropped in next to her, more frustrated with his wife than he was with the SEC. She couldn't go slumming backstage at the Met. They'd both be the laughingstock of Manhattan.

He knew he was too angry to argue further tonight, but this conversation was far from over.

He switched off the lamp next to his bed and heard the beep of her digital thermometer. His head hit the pillow, and he closed his eyes.

Her light stayed on. She didn't move. He couldn't even hear her breathing.

He turned and opened his eyes, blinking at her profile in the lamplight, trying to figure out if she was too upset to sleep.

She twisted her neck to look at him, distress clouding her expression. "I'm ovulating."

Reed's stomach clenched. He only just stopped himself from cursing out loud.

Of all the asinine timing.

How could people be expected to live like this?

"Right," he said with a nod, keeping his voice as controlled as possible.

He slid closer to her, reached over her and turned off her lamp, slipping the thermometer out of her hand to place it on the nightstand.

They'd made love hundreds, maybe thousands of times. They could do it now. Piece of cake.

He left his arm draped around her and burrowed his face into the crook of her neck, inhaling deeply. Once, twice, three times, giving them both a chance to get used to the idea of making love.

Her hair was soft against his cheek, and he ran his hand through it, letting his subconscious kick in and memories wash over him. Her scent was one of the first things he'd loved about her. He remembered dancing under the stars, on the cruise in the harbor, the warm June winds flowing over them as she swayed in his arms in that red dress.

Two minutes into the dance, he knew. He knew he was going to love her, knew he was going to marry her, knew he was going to spend the rest of his life taking care of this funny, gorgeous, intoxicating woman.

Now, he kissed the tender skin of her neck. He trailed his fingertips down the satin of her gown, pressing his warm palm against her abdomen. He kissed her shoulder, her collarbone, then moved to her earlobe, drawing the soft flesh between his lips.

He wanted to tell her he loved her, but things were too tenuous between them. He was building a fragile peace, a respite in the midst of the tough conversation that would have to take place in the next few days. He couldn't hope for more than that.

He fluttered his fingertips along the curve of her waist, up her ribcage, skimming the side of her breast. Desire was slowly but surely thickening his blood. He could feel his breathing deepen and the stirrings of need work their way though his body.

He stroked her shoulder, slipping off the strap of her

gown. Then he made his way down her arm, over her wrist, intending to twine their fingers together as one.

But he found a fist.

A tense, tightly clasped fist.

He jerked back to look at her face.

Her eyes were scrunched tight, her forehead creased and her jaw clenched shut.

"Son of a bitch!" He vaulted off the bed.

Her eyes few open, and he was horrified at the grit, determination and aversion in their depths.

He was *not* forcing himself on a martyr. No matter what the cause, no matter what the rationale.

"This is a marriage," he choked out, "not some stud farm."

He grabbed his bathrobe, striding for the guest bedroom.

Alone in the bed, Elizabeth had cried herself to sleep. She'd wanted to make love, wanted desperately to make a baby. But their argument had replayed over and over in her mind while Reed caressed her, until it had shrouded her love for him, and his touch had felt empty.

She knew it would go away. Intellectually, she knew that only minutes or hours would have to pass before she felt secure in his arms once again. But she'd needed some time before lovemaking.

She'd finally fallen asleep in the early morning hours. Then she woke to the sound of the vacuum, and she knew their housekeeper had arrived, and Reed had gone to work.

Part of her couldn't believe he'd left without waking her to make love. But then she remembered his expression as he'd stormed out of the bedroom. She'd angered him. And maybe she'd hurt him. He had, after all, tried valiantly to put the fight behind them and make love.

She was the one who had failed.

She flipped off the covers, showered, dressed and took her car to the Wellington International office tower on Fifth Avenue.

She rode the elevator to the executive floor and paced through the marble foyer without giving herself a chance to hesitate. She'd apologize to Reed. Not for the fight, but for staying so emotional afterward. She was past it now, and she'd tell him so.

If worst came to worst, she'd flash the lacy black camisole she was wearing under her coat dress. She had thigh-high stockings to match, and she'd put on the skimpiest, sexiest pair of panties she could find in her drawer. She wasn't above a little seduction. And there was a fine hotel right across the street.

"Elizabeth." Reed's secretary, Devon, rose from her chair. She shot a quick, uncertain glance at the window through to Reed's corner office. "Is Reed expecting you?"

"It's a surprise," Elizabeth admitted. She hoped a good surprise.

Devon shot another glance at his office, and there was something strange in her expression. "Let me give him a call."

Elizabeth glanced through the window and saw a woman's profile. She had spiky black hair and wore a dark blazer.

"You wife is here," Devon said into the phone.

There was a split second's delay, and then the woman

shot a guilty glance through the window at Elizabeth. She immediately came to her feet.

"Who's that?" Elizabeth asked Devon.

"She's a job applicant," Devon replied, busying herself with some papers on top of her desk.

Something in the atmosphere made Elizabeth feel awkward. "I hope I'm not disturbing something."

"I'm sure it's fine," said Devon.

The door to Reed's office opened, and the woman came out first. She was a strong, no-nonsense type, about five foot seven, with short cropped hair, classic clothes and a self-confident stride.

She nodded to Elizabeth as she passed, leaving a clean hint of a coconut shampoo in her wake.

"I wasn't expecting you," said Reed, and Elizabeth turned back to face her husband.

"Surprise," said Elizabeth, with a smile for Devon's benefit.

He gestured to the open office door, and she preceded him inside.

"Sorry to disturb you," she offered as he latched the door.

"Not a problem." He indicated a pair of leather chairs in one corner of the room, bracketing a low table.

"Who was she?" Elizabeth asked.

Reed waited for her to sit down. "Who?"

"The woman who just left. Devon said—"

"She's a client," Reed said hurriedly.

Elizabeth froze, a terrible feeling creeping into her empty stomach. He was lying. Why was he lying?

"What kind of a client?"

Reed waved a dismissive hand. "She owns a chain of furniture stores on the West Coast."

Elizabeth nodded, depression settling on her shoulders.

"Did you need something?" Reed asked, tone formal and polite.

I need my husband back.

She was suddenly at a loss. Did she make the proposition? Did she carry on with the seduction plan? Could she bring herself to make love with him knowing he was lying?

"Sweetheart?" he prompted, his tone more intimate.

"I felt bad about last night." She made her decision in a rush.

"The job?"

She shook her head. "The…other."

"Oh."

She grasped her purse with both hands. "I was thinking, maybe we could…" She glanced around, moistening her dry lips. "Make up for lost time."

He blinked at her.

She forced herself to boldly keep his gaze.

"You're not seriously suggesting we make love *here?*"

"The Oak Castle." She named the hotel across the street.

He glanced at his watch.

"Should I have made an appointment?" she asked tightly.

"Gage and Trent are due in ten minutes."

"Cancel."

"Elizabeth." He held up his palms.

"It's time, Reed."

"It'll wait until tonight."

"But we should have done it *last night*." The words were out before she could think about how they sounded.

"Yeah," he agreed, his gaze going hard. "We should have."

She stood then, feeling supremely stupid for having dug out her black lingerie for a workaholic husband. She didn't know why she had expected today to be any different from other days. Reed was a busy man. He fit her in when he could fit her in, and she'd best not ask for more than that.

He immediately stood with her.

"Goodbye then," she offered, turning for the door, struggling to cope with the hurt of his rejection.

But before she could take a step, an unruly little voice urged her to show him what he'd missed. She fought it for a moment, but then decided to get the last word.

Popping the four buttons on her dress, she turned back and jerked it open.

Reed's eyes went wide and he sucked in an involuntary breath.

"Enjoy your meeting," she told him, redoing the buttons, flouncing out of the office and closing the door before he found his voice.

On impulse, she stopped at Devon's desk. "What was the job?" she asked.

Devon looked confused.

"The woman Reed was interviewing. What was the job?"

"Oh." Devon paused. "Accounting."

"Thanks."

"No problem."

Elizabeth marched to the elevator, meeting Gage and Trent coming the other way. At least the part about the meeting with them was true. Elizabeth didn't know what she would have done if he'd lied about everything.

The elevator doors closed, and the express car whooshed smoothly downward. Truth was, she didn't know what she was going to do about any of it at all. Reed was lying to her. He was lying to her about a woman. She seemed like a woman of substance rather than style, and Elizabeth couldn't help but note the contrast between them.

Four

Frustration was evident on the face of Reed Anton Wellington II, "Anton" to his close friends, "Mr. Wellington" or "Sir" to most, and "Father" to Reed.

"And you're saying Kendrick never called, never suggested, never even hinted—"

"Never," Reed confirmed, closing the library door in his parents' Long Island mansion. "Not once, not ever."

"It's things like this that can impact the firm."

"I know that, Father."

"It's things like this that can lose millions of dollars."

"I know that, too." Did Reed's father honestly think the broader impact of the SEC investigation were lost on Reed?

Anton moved behind his desk. "You have a good lawyer? You'll cooperate fully?"

"Of course I'll cooperate fully. I have nothing to hide."

Anton stared silently from beneath bushy eyebrows, and a frightening thought percolated in Reed's mind.

"You know I have nothing to hide, right?"

"You wouldn't be the first to succumb to temptation."

Reed was stunned to hear the words from his own father's mouth. "You think I would cheat?"

"I think you have a lot of pride. I think you're very driven to succeed."

"Wonder where I got that from," Reed muttered.

"I need to know what we're dealing with," said Anton.

Reed took a step toward the wide desk. "We're dealing with an innocent man accused of insider trading, and a ten million dollar blackmail attempt."

"Can you prove the blackmail?"

"I'm the third person in my building to be a victim."

"That's not proof."

"No, but the police are working on it. If they find the blackmailer, the SEC will most certainly drop the charges."

"Do they need more manpower?"

Reed shook his head. "I have my own investigation underway, and Collin's put together a legal team."

"Never was too fond of Collin."

"He graduated top of his class in Harvard Law."

"On a scholarship."

"Father, people who receive scholarships are every bit as capable as those who donate them."

Anton harrumphed. "Genetics isn't nothing."

"Don't go there," Reed warned.

"How is Elizabeth?"

Reed threw up his hands. "I swear to you, I am walking out that door."

"I just asked a question."

"You just linked Elizabeth with the middle class. Therefore, in your opinion poor genetics. Don't try to deny it."

"All right. I won't deny it. How is she?"

Sexy as hell, frustrated as hell, probably mad as hell since it was nearly eight-thirty and Reed wasn't home yet. "She's fine."

Anton moved to the wide, oak bar and uncorked a decanter of scotch. "You mother and I keep waiting for you to announce that you're expecting."

"I know you do."

When he had two fingers of scotch in each crystal glass, Anton turned back. "Any particular reason why you're not?"

"We'll have children when we're ready."

"Your mother's anxious."

"Mother's been anxious since I was eighteen."

"And now you're thirty-four." He handed Reed a glass of scotch. "You can see why the situation is getting worse."

Reed tried to imagine himself explaining the fertility issues to either of his parents. But he couldn't make the picture form in his brain. Not that he would compromise Elizabeth's privacy in any case, especially not to his parents. She was already intimidated by their opinion of anyone outside their tax bracket.

He downed the single malt. "I have to get home."

"I can have somebody from Preston Gautier sit down with Collin."

"Collin's fine," said Reed. "It's all under control."

At least the SEC investigation was under control. The same couldn't be said of the blackmail. And the same certainly couldn't be said of his current situation with Elizabeth.

Reed could still picture the sexy underwear she'd flashed him in his office. If his meeting had been about anything other than her security and the blackmail case, he'd have chased after her like an eager pup. He'd considered doing it anyway. But then Gage and Trevor arrived, and the real world had closed in.

Elizabeth was on her third margarita in Hanna's downtown loft, blocking out the real world and taking the edge off her humiliation.

"You actually flashed him?" Hanna's laugh was rife with disbelief. "Right there in the Wellington International office?"

"I was wearing underwear," Elizabeth pointed out, stretching out on her stomach on Hanna's leather couch. Hanna was already lounging sideways in an armchair, her shoes kicked off, feet swaying, the slushy drink dangling from her fingers.

"Ever done anything like that before?"

Elizabeth shook her head.

"Bet he was surprised."

Elizabeth nearly giggled at the memory. "I'm pretty sure he was speechless."

"I bet."

Elizabeth's smile faded. She realized the margaritas must be strong or she wouldn't be finding any of this even remotely funny. "I think I was jealous."

"Of what?"

Elizabeth took another sip of the drink. "Okay, this is going to sound crazy. But there was an attractive woman in his office when I got there. He lied about her." She sat up, swinging her feet around to the floor. "He told me she was a client. Devon told me she was a job applicant."

"Uh-oh." Hanna's swinging feet came to a halt.

A few beats went by in silence.

"You think he's having an affair?" asked Elizabeth.

"I absolutely do not," Hanna said with conviction.

"Why would he lie?"

"This is Reed we're talking about. He is not screwing around on his wife."

"Reed's human."

"You have one lie. One little lie, that might not even be a lie. What if Devon made a mistake? What if she thought the mystery woman was a job applicant, and she really was a client?"

"Devon is a crackerjack assistant. She doesn't make mistakes like that."

"Still," said Hanna. "The evidence is way too flimsy to start thinking infidelity."

"What about this?" Elizabeth stood, struggling with her balance for a split second. "Pretend you're a man." She flicked open one of the buttons on her dress. "You're a man, and you haven't had sex in three weeks." She flicked another. "Your wife—your ovulating wife—walks into your office." She flicked the last two. "And flashes this."

Elizabeth opened the coat dress to reveal her sexy lingerie ensemble.

"Wow," said Hanna in obvious awe.

Elizabeth closed the dress. "Does it take a team of wild oxen to keep you away from me? Or is a routine meeting enough to do it?"

"Wild oxen," said Hanna. "Damn, you're in good shape."

"It's the spa membership, my personal trainer."

"I want to join that spa."

Both women went silent as Elizabeth buttoned up and sat back down.

"I still think you're wrong," said Hanna.

Elizabeth desperately wanted to believe Hanna. But there was a sick feeling deep down in her soul that warned her something was going on.

Just then, her cell phone chimed on the table, and she saw it was Reed. She made no move to answer.

"He must be wondering where you are," said Hanna.

"Let him wonder." It chimed again.

"He'll be worried."

"Serves him right."

Hanna moved from the chair and sat down next to her. "Promise me something?"

It chimed a third time.

"What?" asked Elizabeth, clasping her hands together, fighting the urge to answer Reed's call.

"Promise me you'll believe it's nothing until it's not." Hanna reached out to squeeze her hands. "He's a good man, Elizabeth. And he loves you."

Elizabeth took a deep breath, nodded, and reached for the phone, pressing the pickup button.

"Hello?"

"Where *are* you?" Reed demanded, his tone catching Elizabeth off guard.

Her softer feelings for him evaporated. "I'm flashing my underwear for somebody who appreciates it."

There was absolute silence on Reed's end.

Hanna snatched the phone from Elizabeth's hand and raised it to her ear. "Reed, it's Hanna. I'm really sorry. I think I gave Elizabeth one too many margaritas." After a pause, she said, "No. I won't let her drive." She handed the phone back to Elizabeth.

"Hello, darling," said Elizabeth, then she hiccupped.

"You're drunk?"

"A little," she admitted. Not that it changed the facts. Reed was in all likelihood cheating on a drunken spouse, that was all.

"I'm sending a car," he told her.

"Are you drunk, too?"

"No, I'm not drunk."

"But you're not coming yourself?"

"I'm in Long Island. I just left my parents'."

"And if I called them?" Elizabeth couldn't help but challenge. Maybe he was in Long Island, or maybe he was holed up in a hotel room somewhere.

"Why would you call them?"

"I don't know. To say hi. Whatever."

"Elizabeth, it's time for you to stop drinking."

"Sure." She was feeling a little dizzy anyway. And a hangover wouldn't help the job search. And, sex or no sex tonight, she was finding herself a job in the morning and getting started on her very own life.

* * *

Reed waited in the lobby for Elizabeth's car to arrive. Henry was behind his desk, looking nervous about something. The man's gaze twitched from Reed, to the back of the lobby, then out to the sidewalk. Strange.

But then the dark sedan pulled up, and Reed hustled through the double doors to meet Elizabeth.

He helped her upstairs and into the penthouse, tossed her coat on the sofa and took her straight through to the bedroom. There he gently laid her back on their bed and slipped off her shoes.

"You know," she sighed, her eyes closed, hair disheveled, one of her sexy stockings drooping down. "It shouldn't be this hard for two married people to have sex."

"No," he agreed. "It shouldn't be this hard." While she lay with her eyes closed, breathing deeply, he gently removed her jewelry and unbuttoned her dress, his breath catching at the sight of her camisole and skimpy panties.

"Reed?"

"Yes?"

"Promise me something?"

He raised his gaze to her sweet, relaxed expression. "Of course."

"If I fall asleep—" She stopped.

"Yes?" he prompted.

"Let's make love anyway."

He shook his head, allowing himself a tired smile. "Like that's going to happen."

"Good," she said with a smile of her own.

He leaned down. "Elizabeth, I'm telling you no."

The smile turned to a frown. "You're always telling me no."

"I never tell you no."

She had him well and truly wrapped around her little finger. There was almost nothing he could deny her.

"I got all dressed up," she complained.

His gaze dipped down to the black lace highlighting her cleavage. "That, you did."

"Hanna said I looked sexy."

He grinned. "Just how drunk are you?"

She giggled. Then she tilted her chin in determination. "I am getting a job."

"We'll talk about that in the morning."

Her expression changed, and she reached out to him. "Please, make me pregnant tonight." And then her arms went limp, slinking down to the bed, and her body relaxed into sleep.

"Not like this," he whispered, smoothing back her hair and kissing her on the forehead. "Never like this."

He gently removed the rest of her clothes, and tucked her under the covers, stepping back to gaze at her beauty and vulnerability. His cell phone rang, and he quickly opened it, afraid of disturbing her. But she didn't even stir.

Still, he kept his voice low and moved out of the room. "Hello?"

"It's Collin. Selina's at my place."

Reed glanced at his watch. Nine-thirty. "Is anything wrong?"

"Can you come down?"

"Why don't you come up here. Elizabeth's asleep."
For some reason, Reed didn't want to leave her alone
right now.

"Good enough. Be right up," said Collin, signing off.

Reed pocketed his cell phone then pulled the bedroom door closed. Odds were, they'd completely missed
their window of opportunity for this month. Because, he
expected it to be twenty-four hours before Elizabeth
was feeling remotely romantic again.

And she'd be upset about that.

Well, he was upset, too.

In fact, he was beginning to feel bone weary. The
blackmail, the murder, the SEC, all the usual problems
at Wellington International. Added to that, his father's
values and the persistent infertility trouble were wearing him down. He needed to fix something, anything.
But he was operating on every front and, so far, it was
to no avail.

For the first time in Reed's life, he wondered if hard
work and ingenuity would be enough.

There was a light knock on the front door, and he
crossed the foyer to answer it, escorting Collin and
Selina to his home office where they took seats around
a polished black table.

Reed directed the conversation. "I thought you had
somebody on Elizabeth," he told Selina.

She looked startled. "I do."

"She went downtown today. I need a report on things
like that."

She jotted down a note in her book. "Sure."

Collin looked at him strangely. "Did something happen while Elizabeth was downtown?" he asked.

"She visited a friend. But I didn't know where she was."

"Just to be clear," Selina added. "Do you want a report on Mrs. Wellington's daily activities or on potential threats?"

Reed took in the expressions on their faces. "I'm not spying on my wife," he protested. But neither did he want her wandering around drunk downtown when there might be a murderer on the loose.

"Perhaps if we changed the nature of the operation," suggested Selina. "Put Joe a little closer to Mrs. Wellington. Say, as her driver? That way, he doesn't have to stay concealed, and he can report to you at intervals."

"I like it," said Reed. "What else do you have?"

"Kendrick," said Collin.

"You found him?"

Collin shook his head. "He's still in Washington, elusive as ever. But some more information has come to light."

"Does it help us?"

Collin and Selina glanced at each other.

"Unfortunately," said Collin, "Hammond and Pysanski also invested in Ellias and made a bundle."

"But, they're—"

"Kendrick's former business partners."

Reed rocked back in his chair.

"It does look pretty bad," said Selina.

Reed couldn't help but defend himself. "Do you

honestly think that if I were going to put together a conspiracy to insider trade, that *this* would be my master plan? A senator giving a heads up on a contract award to four of his closest associates, hoping nobody would notice? It's lame-ass. It's beyond stupid."

Collin leaned forward, eyes hard as he mimicked Reed. "'I'm a smarter criminal than that, Your Honor.' Is that really going to be the cornerstone of your defense?"

"You got a better one?"

"Not at the moment. But if I don't come up with something better than that, Harvard Law School wasted a lot of time and money on me."

"I want this behind me," Reed growled. "There are problems cropping up in the Irish merger, and Germany is talking about changing their safety standards. I don't have time for distractions."

"I'm meeting with the SEC tomorrow," said Selina.

"Take Collin with you."

Something twitched in her expression.

"What?" asked Reed.

She hesitated. "Sometimes Collin cramps my style."

Reed felt his hands curl involuntarily into fists. "There are problems between you two?"

"Stylistic differences," said Collin.

"I take a tough stance. He undermines it."

Reed glanced from one to the other. "You're kidding me?" With all they were facing, these two couldn't get together on their interview techniques?

"Work it out. I want you both in that meeting."

Selina's gaze slid to Collin. He nodded, then so did she.

"Have Joe stop at the office in the morning," said Reed, wrapping things up. "I'll bring him by and introduce him to Elizabeth."

Morning was not kind to Elizabeth.

Rain spattered on the penthouse roof, tapping against her bedroom balcony doors, pounding its way into her fragile skull. She pulled the comforter over her head, praying her housekeeper, Rena, wasn't planning to vacuum today.

Slamming back margaritas on an empty stomach had obviously been a bad idea. It had been a few years since Elizabeth had gotten drunk. And, right now, she was sure it would be many more years before she indulged in more than two drinks in an evening. She blinked open one bleary eye, squinting at the alarm clock. Nine-fifty-two.

She spotted a large glass of water on the nightstand. Sitting next to it were two aspirin tablets. Bless Reed.

She wiggled herself into a sitting position and took the pills. If she could sleep until they kicked in, she'd have a fighting chance of surviving this hangover.

Bless Reed, she thought again. She could forgive him anything at the moment. Well, almost anything.

Though, in the cold light of day, she realized it was unlikely he was having an affair. It wasn't so much her confidence in the strength of their relationship. It was more her knowledge of his core values and principles.

Reed wouldn't cheat.

Even if he wanted to cheat, his honor and principles wouldn't let him.

The rain pulsed harder on the window. She pressed her fingers into her ears and buried her face in the feather pillow, conjuring images of the night before.

Hanna had blended up some fine margaritas, and she'd handed out some sage and practical advice. Plus, it had felt just plain good for Elizabeth to get her anxiety off her chest.

But then Reed had called and annoyed her. Still, when he'd helped her to bed, she'd remembered all the reasons she'd fallen in love with him in the first place. So she'd propositioned him, because time was running out.

Now, she groaned. Time really was running out, and she had no memory past asking to make love last night. She was pretty sure she'd remember it if it had happened.

So, she wasn't pregnant. And it was day three of ovulation. But she didn't think she could even drag herself out of bed at the moment, never mind seduce her husband.

Thunder rumbled in the distance, and the downpour turned torrential. But slowly, ever so slowly, the sound of the raindrops stopped hurting her brain. They became soothing, and the pain went from sharp to dull.

She drifted in and out for an hour, then forced herself to throw off the covers, pulling gingerly into a sitting position. She was tired, but at least she was mobile.

She showered and dressed, and applied a little concealer to disguise the dark circles under her eyes.

She wasn't quite ready for a workout at the gym, but she needed to get the blood flowing somehow. The rain was steady, so a walk was out of the question. She needed to find something to do inside.

The penthouse was empty. Rena was likely out running errands and would be home soon. She didn't like it when Elizabeth cleaned. Baking was acceptable, but baking would fill the suite with aromas.

Not good.

Elizabeth glanced around for inspiration. She caught sight of the living room bookshelf. There was an idea. She could sort through her books, maybe donate some of the older ones to the library. And Reed had hundreds shelved in his office. She'd call Rena on her cell and get her to pick up some cardboard boxes on her way home.

Perfect.

After gathering a sizable pile in the living room, she moved to the office.

Reed liked the occasional mystery or thriller, the kind of book that you didn't reread once you knew the ending. She tugged a couple of his volumes from the eye level shelves and carried them to the black meeting table.

There she paused, wrinkling her nose, trying to identify an unusual smell. It wasn't dust, not leather, not furniture polish. Where had she…

Coconut.

She staggered back in shock.

That woman in Reed's office had smelled of coconut.

"Elizabeth?" Reed called from the entry hall.

The coconut woman had been in the penthouse? Her penthouse? Her home?

"What's with the books?"

She could hear his footsteps starting down the hall.

What did she do? Ignore it? Confront him? Look for more evidence?

Was this why he hadn't made love with her last night? Or yesterday? Or last week?

"There you are." He came around the corner and smiled. "Feeling okay?"

She stared at him in silence, trying to reconcile the man she knew with such reprehensible behavior. While she was desperately trying to save their marriage, had he already ended it?

"There's somebody I want you to meet," said Reed, coming fully into the room.

Not her. Good grief, not her.

"This is Joe Germain."

A man came into view in the doorway, and Reed motioned him into the office.

"Joe, this is my wife, Elizabeth Wellington."

The man stepped forward. He was at least six foot three, with broad shoulders, a burly chest, and very little in the way of a neck. His hair was cropped close, and he wore a dark, neat suit with a dress shirt and tie.

"A pleasure to meet you, Mrs. Wellington." The man held out a strong, callused hand.

"Hello," Elizabeth managed, giving a brief shake, catching a glimpse of a leather holster beneath his suit jacket. Then she met gray eyes, intelligent eyes, some might even say cunning.

"I've hired Joe as your driver," Reed continued.

A driver?

Elizabeth might have been duped, but she wasn't stupid. The man looked like he was half linebacker, half mercenary. He definitely wasn't somebody she'd want to be alone with in a dark alley.

A visceral chill worked its way up her spine.

"Elizabeth?" Reed's confused voice seemed to come from a long way off. "Are you okay?"

She looked back to her husband, her lying, cheating, untrustworthy husband. "I don't need a driver."

Five

"Elizabeth," said Hanna, her voice chastising as she dunked a tea bag into the teapot at her counter. "You have seriously gone round the bend."

"He insisted, absolutely *insisted* I keep the guy as my driver." Elizabeth had tried every argument in the book to change Reed's mind, but his stubbornness had been off the charts, even for him.

"Maybe he simply wants you to have a driver. You did get pretty drunk last night."

"That guy is *not* a driver."

"He drove you here, didn't he?"

Only because Elizabeth had been too frightened to try to escape. "I think he's a criminal."

"Now, why on earth would Reed hire a criminal?"

Elizabeth hesitated, reluctant to give voice to the fear that had followed her over. But she had to share it with someone. "What if they're right?"

"Who?" Hanna returned to the living area of her loft, where rain pattered on the skylights, and dull daylight gave the airy room a gray atmosphere.

"The SEC. What if Reed has a secret life? What if his wealth really *is* from shady deals with the under-world?" Her mouth went dry and her voice shook ever so slightly. "You know, he's got an awful lot of money."

Hanna enunciated slowly and carefully. "Round the bend, Elizabeth. Reed is a husband and a businessman."

But there were too many inconsistencies lately. He was being far too secretive for this to all be nothing. "Not that much of a husband," Elizabeth pointed out. "He's fooling around with the coconut woman."

"You don't know that he's fooling around with the coconut woman."

"He lied about her. And I know she was in our suite." Elizabeth warmed to the theory. "You know, my parents warned me about rich people. They said they were sly and untrustworthy. They were rich for a reason, and it wasn't hard work and fair trade practices."

"Elizabeth."

"What?"

"You disagree with your parents on that, remember?"

"I was wrong. And look where it got me."

Hanna fought a grin. "You mean with the imagina-tion of a conspiracy theorist? Forget being a script girl. You might want to consider script*writing* as your future career."

"What future career? I'll probably be killed in gang-land crossfire before I can ever get a career off the ground. I might know too much already."

"This is insane," said Hanna, picking up her phone. "What's his name?"

"Reed Anton Wellington III."

Hanna shot her a look of dark disbelief. "I mean your driver."

"Oh. Joe Germain. What are you doing?"

"I'm calling Bert Ralston. You give an investigative reporter an hour, and you'll be amazed what he can find out."

Elizabeth plunked back on the couch. That wasn't a half bad idea. At least then Hanna would believe her. At least then Elizabeth would know if she was in any danger from Joe.

How could Reed do this to her? She'd been an innocent young college graduate from New Hampshire when he met her, wooed her, enticed her away from the safe bosom of her family. She never should have borrowed that red dress, or gone on the harbor cruise. Then she never would have met Reed.

Hanna hung up the phone. "You know, you were a lot more fun last night when you were drunk."

"You're not taking this seriously enough," Elizabeth accused.

Hanna rose to pour the tea. "I'm taking this exactly seriously enough. You want vanilla cookies?"

Elizabeth's stomach gave a little lurch of protest. "How come you're not hung over?" she asked Hanna, rising to follow her into the kitchen area.

"Because you outdrank me. How are you feeling by the way?"

"You mean other than facing imminent death by either criminal gang wars or by annoying my driver?"

Hanna carefully poured two cups of steaming tea. "Yeah."

"Bit of a headache. Reed left me some aspirins on the nightstand."

"Yet more evidence of his evil cold-bloodedness."

"He didn't want me to suspect anything."

"Well, that's not working out so well for him so far, is it?"

"That's because of my brilliant, deductive mind."

"It's because of your pickle-brained paranoia."

"I heard the lies. I smelled the coconut."

Hanna's telephone rang and Elizabeth cringed.

Hanna picked it up. "Hello?" She looked at Elizabeth and mouthed *Bert Ralston.* She listened for a moment. Then her brows shot up. "Really?"

"What?" Elizabeth demanded in a stage whisper. Her heart rate deepened in her chest.

"Okay," said Hanna. "Thanks. I owe you one." And she hung up the phone.

"Well?" asked Elizabeth, easing into a chair, because the feeling had suddenly left her legs.

"Joe Germain isn't a driver."

A loud clanging grew inside Elizabeth's head.

"He's a bodyguard."

"What?"

"He's a bodyguard, Lizzy. He works for a national

agency called Resolute Charter. Reed's not trying to hurt you, he's trying to protect you."

An instant rush of relief shot through Elizabeth's body.

For a split second, it masked all the other questions.

But then they percolated back. "Protect me from *what?*"

"I'm guessing reporters. With Hammond and Pysanski's involvement, this SEC thing is heating up."

Elizabeth had no idea who Hammond and Pysanski were. But Reed wasn't a member of a criminal gang. And her life as she knew it hadn't just ended.

"It doesn't explain the coconut woman," she pointed out.

Hanna slid down into a chair beside her. "If you give it a little time, I'll bet the coconut woman explains herself."

"Dad called here looking for an explanation."

Elizabeth was delighted to hear her brother Brandon's deep voice on the other end of the phone.

"Why didn't he call *me?*" She crossed the living room to curl up in her favorite wingback chair next to the bay window. The clouds were still gray, but the rain had turned to drizzle.

"He thinks the FBI has your phone bugged."

"It's the SEC, and they don't bug phones."

Did they?

If they did, maybe she could get her hands on the tapes and get some information on coconut woman.

"You holding up okay?" asked Brandon.

Elizabeth traced a zigzag pattern on the smooth leather arm. "I'm fine."

Truth was, the SEC was far from her biggest problem at the moment.

"So, you're not worried?" asked Brandon.

"He's got a good lawyer, and they say it's going well." As she finished the sentence, she realized that Reed hadn't in fact said a single thing to her about the case since their initial discussion. In truth, she had no idea how it was going.

"How are things in California?" she asked brightly.

"I hired another vet last week," said Brandon. "And we're advertising for two technicians."

"Business is booming?"

"The practice is definitely growing. We're not in your tax bracket yet, but Heather has her eye on a little house up the coast."

"You're selling the condo?"

"With a growing family—"

"Heather's pregnant again?" Elizabeth hated the pain that filled her chest at the thought of Heather having another baby. She would be thrilled to be an auntie a second time. Babies were nothing but good news. Even if they weren't hers.

"No, Heather's not pregnant. Lucas isn't even a year old."

"Right." Elizabeth was ashamed of her reaction.

"Lizzy?"

"Uh-huh?" She promised herself she'd do better when her sister-in-law really was pregnant.

"I'm sorry you're not conceiving."

Everything inside Elizabeth went still, and a lump instantly formed in her throat. "How did you…?"

Brandon's voice went low and protective, and suddenly they were teenagers again, sharing secrets, laughing and conspiring. "I saw it in your eyes when Heather was pregnant. Then again when you held Lucas. And I hear it in your voice every time we talk about children."

"We're trying," she managed.

"I know. And I assume you have the best medical care money can buy?"

She nodded, then uttered a weak, "Yes."

"It'll happen, Lizzy."

"How long—" Elizabeth stopped herself. It was none of her business.

"Did Heather take to conceive?"

"Yes."

"A couple of months."

Elizabeth reflexively wrapped an arm across her stomach, leaning slightly forward in the chair. She and Reed had been trying for three years.

"I predict," Brandon said into the silence, "that not too long from now, you'll be sitting in my house with a plump, smiling baby wrapped in your arms, and you'll be saying to me 'Thank goodness it took so long. Otherwise we wouldn't have Johnny or Sally or Mary or Tim—the most perfect baby in the world.'"

Elizabeth's throat was so tight, she couldn't speak.

"Lizzy?"

"Three *years*," she moaned, saying it out loud for the first time, feeling the weight of all those failed cycles pressing down on her shoulders.

"It'll happen."

"And what if it doesn't?"

"It's way too early for contingency plans. Trust me. I'm a doctor."

"You're a veterinarian."

"And I spend an enormous amount of my time consulting on breeding issues—dogs, cats, horses, goats."

"I'm not a goat."

"Principle's the same."

There was a muffled rustle on the other end of the phone.

"Elizabeth?" came Heather's breathless voice.

Mortification flushed Elizabeth's body. "You heard?"

"Yes. And I'm about to kill your brother."

Brandon's protest was faint in the background. "I wasn't saying she was a goat."

"Shut up," Heather instructed Brandon. To Elizabeth, she said, "There are plenty of choices."

"I really didn't want this to become—"

"Since you're still trying, I assume Reed's not sterile?"

Elizabeth worked her jaw, but no sound came out.

Heather's voice went muffled. "Of course we can talk about it. We're family. You go check on Lucas."

Her voice came back on the receiver. "Have you tried in vitro fertilization?"

"Uh…no," Elizabeth admitted.

"Artificial insemination? With Reed's sperm, of course."

Once she got past the shock, Elizabeth realized there was something strangely comforting about Heather's matter-of-fact approach. "I've been taking my temperature."

"That's good. Elevate your hips, and don't move for half an hour afterward."

"Right," said Elizabeth, wondering just how far this conversation would go.

Heather's voice went low. "Brandon doesn't know it, but I took my temperature for six months before we tried for Lucas. I knew exactly when I was ovulating. I mean, why take chances?"

"Did you hold off on sex?" Elizabeth could hardly believe she'd asked the question.

"We did. For a little over a week. Of course, Brandon didn't know what I was up to, so he got a little frustrated and confused." Heather laughed. "Never had so many headaches in my life."

Elizabeth smiled, finding the knot in her stomach easing off. "And it worked."

"Like a charm."

"It hasn't for me."

"Nature is fickle," said Heather. "It might take time. And, as for contingency plans, if nothing else works, we'll take your eggs and Reed's sperm, and I'll grow a baby for you."

"What?" Elizabeth coughed out, certain she couldn't have heard properly.

"I'll be your surrogate mother," said Heather with conviction. "We already know I grow the best babies in the world."

Elizabeth's chest filled with emotion, and her eyes welled up with tears. "I don't… You couldn't…"

"Oh yes, I could. And I will."

Elizabeth's sob was audible. She was completely

beyond words. Heather had just made the most generous, kind-spirited offer a human being could make.

"Lizzy, you're my sister, and I love you. And I want you to know that you're a million miles away from exhausting your options." She paused. "Okay?"

Elizabeth nodded, still unable to speak.

"I'm going to take that as a yes."

"I love you, too," Elizabeth whispered.

"Can you come to visit? Is Reed allowed to leave the state?"

The question surprised a laugh out of Elizabeth. "Yes, he's allowed to leave the state.

"Good. Let's make some plans."

"Sure. Yeah. Okay."

"Oops. Lucas is crying. Looks like Daddy's blowing it in there. Bye for now. We'll see you soon!"

Then Heather was gone. And Elizabeth sat staring numbly at the telephone. Her sister-in-law was an angel. She was a saint. And somehow her strength and kindness made Elizabeth feel pathetic.

Elizabeth had once been strong. She'd once had the world at her feet. She was fit and attractive. She had a college degree and a husband to die for. She'd had confidence and energy, and a sense of optimism that told her everything was going to turn out well.

But it hadn't.

And now she had no children, no career, and potentially no husband.

She pictured Reed, wondering what, or who, he was doing right now. Then she banished the vision, remembering Hanna's advice instead. It wasn't reasonable to assume he was having an affair.

It was reasonable, however, to wonder if he was coming home for dinner. She pressed the on button on the phone and dialed his office number.

It rang four times before Devon picked up. "Reed Wellington's office."

"Hi, Devon. It's just me."

"Oh. Hi, Elizabeth." Was there something in her voice? "He just left for a dinner meeting."

A dinner meeting? Was that suspicious? Was he with *her?* "Do you know which restaurant?"

Devon hesitated. "I…"

Damn. It *was* suspicious. "Never mind. I know I wrote it down this morning," Elizabeth lied. "I think it was Reno's…maybe The Bridge…"

"Alexander's," Devon put in.

"Oh, yes. Alexander's. Thanks," Elizabeth said as cheerfully as she could manage, then she hung up and pulled a business card out of her blazer pocket.

Reasonable or not, she dialed Joe Germain's cell phone.

"Might as well make yourself useful," she mumbled while it rang through. It was impossible to get a parking spot near Alexander's at this time of day.

Joe was at her door in less than a minute.

"How'd you do that?" she asked, letting him into the foyer while she slipped on a coat.

"Do what, ma'am?"

"Get here so fast."

"I was in the lobby."

"Lurking?"

One corner of his mouth flexed. "Pretty much."

She hooked her purse over her shoulder. "Is that what you do?"

"Excuse me, ma'am?"

The door closed behind them, and she pulled out her key to lock the dead bolt. "When you're not driving. Do you simply lurk in the lobby?"

"Sometimes I wash the car." He followed her toward the elevator.

"And shoot the bad guys?"

He reached out and pressed the elevator button but didn't answer.

"I know you have a gun," she told him.

"I do have a gun, ma'am."

"Call me Elizabeth. Why do you have a gun?"

"Because this is New York City."

The elevator car arrived, and he gestured for her to go first.

"I know you're not a driver."

"I am a driver, ma'am."

"Elizabeth."

He gave her a look that said her first name wouldn't be passing over his lips anytime soon. "Mrs. Wellington."

"I know you're my bodyguard."

Again, he didn't answer.

"I take it you can neither confirm nor deny you were hired as my bodyguard?"

They started across the lobby.

"Where would you like to go?" he asked in a cool, professional voice.

"I'll pretend I don't know," she offered. "But I think you and I should be straight with one another."

"Am I taking you to dinner? To run errands?"

"Isn't there some kind of special bond? Bodyguard and protectee? One that calls for complete honesty? Considering you may be throwing yourself in front of a bullet for me?"

Joe gave a small sigh. "Visiting a friend?"

"Spying on my husband."

Joe stopped dead.

She took two more steps and then turned and fluttered her lashes. "Is that a conflict of interest for you?"

"No." He started walking again.

"Good. Alexander's Restaurant, please."

Reed paused in the foyer of Alexander's, grateful that Selina's informant had been right.

Third booth past the wine cellar, partially screened by a white, marble pillar, there was Senator Kendrick. He was flanked by two gorgeous young women, and there was an open bottle of Romanée-Conti on the table. No surprise there. The senator was a fairly infamous womanizer. Not that Reed cared one way or the other. The senator's personal life was his own business.

Reed strode confidently past the maître d', rounded the end of the polished bar and came upon Kendrick before the man had a chance to spot him.

"Good evening, Senator." Without waiting for an invitation, Reed slipped into the burgundy velvet booth, sliding up next to the blond woman, helping himself to a breadstick.

The senator's expression faltered, but the woman immediately curved her red lips into a welcoming smile, and she draped a long-fingered hand on Reed's shoulder.

A waiter appeared at the table. "Would you care for a drink, sir? Some wine?"

"Macallan eighteen-year-old," said Reed. "One ice cube."

The waiter nodded and withdrew.

"Reed," Kendrick finally acknowledged with a nod.

"Back from Washington?" Reed asked.

"This afternoon."

"I've been trying to get hold of you."

"I got your messages."

"And?"

"And my lawyers have advised me not to speak publicly on the matter."

Reed cracked the breadstick in half. "Where my lawyers have advised me to *convince* you to speak publicly on the matter."

Kendrick's bushy-browed eyes narrowed.

"I was surprised to read about Hammond and Pysanski." Reed let his gaze bore into the man he'd known and trusted for a dozen years. Not that Kendrick would be the first politician to go bad.

"As was I."

"Something I should know?" asked Reed.

"Should we powder our noses, Michael?" asked the brunette woman.

"No," said Kendrick. "Mr. Wellington won't be staying long."

The waiter set Reed's drink down on the white tablecloth. Then he topped up the others' wineglasses and removed the bottle.

"Reed *Wellington?*" asked the blond woman.

"In the flesh," Reed responded, giving her a brief, polite smile.

"I saw you in the paper just this morning." She sidled a little closer, her arm stretching out along the back of the bench seat. "You're much better looking in color and three dimensions."

Reed took a sip of the scotch, putting his focus on Kendrick. "Do you have something to hide?"

"What do you think?"

"I think Hammond and Pysanski were a very unexpected turn of events."

"That makes me guilty?"

"That makes *me look guilty.*" Reed enunciated each word.

"You go down, I go down," said Kendrick.

"Trent says we get out front of it."

Kendrick shook his head. "I don't want to close any doors."

"What about the other?" Reed didn't have to mention the murder and blackmail for Kendrick to get the point. "I want my family safe, and the more information you can provide—"

"Can't help you there." But there was something in Kendrick's eyes. Something Reed couldn't quite put his finger on. Would Kendrick have to take the Fifth? Was the SEC actually on to something?

Reed downed the drink. "This isn't going to sit well with my board of directors."

"Yeah," Kendrick snorted. "Because losing the Wellington International campaign contribution is my biggest worry right now."

"*Do* you have a biggest worry right now?"

"You mean other than the SEC charges?"

"Of which we're innocent." Reed watched closely for a reaction.

"Like that matters." Kendrick pasted him with a forbidding stare. "You read the papers. You follow the news. Who doesn't want to see a corrupt senator and billionaire go to jail?"

Reed spun his crystal tumbler. "Yeah? Well, I hear you can greatly reduce your chances of being incarcerated simply by not committing a crime."

"That's always been my first line of defense," said Kendrick.

"Then let Trent videotape your statement."

Kendrick shook his head. "No can do."

"I'm going to find out why," Reed warned. He waited a beat, but Kendrick didn't respond.

Then he shoved his glass to the middle of the table and rose to his feet.

Six

Home from the enlightening stop at Alexander's, Elizabeth stood in her kitchen and struggled to remember the last time she and Reed had eaten in their dining room. Rena was also a cook, and when they were first married, she would make sumptuous four- or five-course dinners. Elizabeth and Reed would indulge in a long, candlelit meal, gazing over the park, talking about the events of the day, their hopes and dreams.

But it had been months since Reed had been home before Rena left for the day. Eventually, the housekeeper had started leaving dinner in the refrigerator for later, tourtière or manicotti—things that were easy to reheat.

Not that Reed would be hungry tonight. Elizabeth was sure he and his little party of four had had a won-

derful dinner at Alexander's. While Elizabeth had settled for a banana and a glass of juice.

A key turned in the lock on the penthouse door, and
her stomach lurched. She'd been tempted to pack her
bags and leave before he arrived. But she kept hearing
Hanna's voice asking her to assume it was nothing until
proven otherwise. Well, Reed was about to prove it one
way or the other.

"Elizabeth?" he called, latching the door shut behind him.

She heard him toss his keys on the entry table, then
his footfalls moved toward the living room. She walked
out of the kitchen to meet him halfway, glancing at the
grandfather clock that showed it was ten-fifteen.

"Tough day?" she asked as he loosened his tie.

"I got stuck in meetings."

"Ahh." She nodded, moving behind the sofa and putting it between them. "With anyone in particular?"

"The last one was with Collin."

"Just Collin?"

Reed peered at her strangely. "Yeah."

"Hmm."

"Have you eaten?"

"Were you at the office?"

He didn't even miss a beat. "Downstairs. Collin's
apartment."

She didn't respond.

"We could order something from Cabo Luca." He
picked up the phone.

"You didn't eat earlier?"

"Not a thing. I'm starved."

Wow. She'd had no idea her husband was such an accomplished liar.

"Any other *meetings* tonight?"

He paused and cocked his head sideways. "What's this curiosity all about?"

"Just making conversation." She ran her fingertips along the back of the sofa. "Wanting to know about my darling husband's day."

"Tell me about your day. Anything new on the anniversary party?"

"We've chosen the napkins." After only three weeks of deliberation between the party planner, the caterer and the florist. Elizabeth couldn't imagine why her life didn't feel completely fulfilling.

"That's good," said Reed.

"Nothing with Senator Kendrick?"

Reed's eyes narrowed. "Why would you ask that?"

She shrugged. "The SEC investigation."

"I told you not to worry about that."

"Well, I am worried about that. I read the papers. Which, by the way, is my only source of information on this subject."

Reed moved toward her, but she backed off a few steps.

"I saw him briefly, earlier today."

"Just Kendrick?"

"Yes. Trent thought it would be good for me to talk to him alone. If you must know, we want him to make a public statement that we're innocent."

A completely inappropriate chuckle burst from Elizabeth. "Innocent?"

"Of course."

Her throat closed in, and her voice rose an octave. "I don't know what the hell you and Kendrick were doing for four hours with those supermodels, but it sure as hell didn't look *innocent* to me."

Reed drew back, his eyes going wide. "Whoa."

"Who were they, Reed? Or do you even remember their names? A month ago, I would have sworn on a stack of Bibles that you were a faithful husband. And then I thought it was one woman. And now I don't know how the hell many. How long? How long have you been living a lie?"

"Elizabeth!" Arms outstretched, he took two steps forward.

She looped around the end of the sofa. "You stay away from me."

"I swear, I have no idea what you're talking about."

"Swear all you want, Reed. Because I know how well you lie."

"I've been completely faithful." His expression was earnest. If she didn't know better, she'd believe him without question.

"Is that why you wouldn't make love with me? Was it because of her?"

"There is no her. I didn't make love with you because you cringed at my touch. Then I was working, and then you were passed out drunk. I want a baby as much as you do, but I'm not making love to an unconscious wife."

"Then maybe you should have one with someone else." She finished the statement on a sob, realizing how very much the thought of Reed having a baby with someone else hurt her. She loved him. Even through all of this, she still loved him.

It was pathetic.

"Who else?" he demanded, and she could see he was growing angry.

Well, so was she. "I don't know. Take your pick. Maybe that blonde who was hanging all over you in the restaurant, or maybe the—"

"I don't know what people told you. But my meeting with the senator was—"

"*Told* me?" She laughed again, slightly shrill, slightly hysterical. "Nobody had to tell me anything. I was there, Reed. I saw you. I saw her."

"How—"

"My driver. Or should I say my bodyguard. Joe from Resolute Charter. The finest protection money can buy. Did you know he had a gun? Wait. How silly of me. Of course he had a gun. Is he protecting me from irate girlfriends?"

"The blond woman was nobody. I didn't even know her name. She was with the senator—"

"Quit lying to me!"

Reed took a giant step forward, wrapping his big hands around her upper arms. He didn't squeeze. He wasn't hurting her, but she also knew he wasn't about to let go.

"I am not lying about the blonde. I saw her for twenty minutes tops. Call and check with Collin if you want.

"Yes, I hired a bodyguard. But he's also a driver. You want to go out in the city? You want to drink with Hanna? You want to hunt for jobs? Fine. But you're going to be safe while you do it.

"I'm under investigation, Elizabeth. I swear to God I'm innocent, and nobody's going to prove otherwise. But the court of public opinion is an entirely different matter. You could be accosted by reporters or self-righteous citizens, or by anybody else on the street. Joe will keep you safe."

A little of the fight went out of Elizabeth. Was there some logic to that rant? He seemed sincere, offended that his morals had been called into question. And he had conceded on the job front.

"You're okay with me finding a job?"

"Not in the least. But if you're going to do it, you're going to do it. You're not my prisoner, Elizabeth. Although some days I wish you were."

Elizabeth suddenly felt exhausted. Sad and exhausted. What was the truth? What were lies? How was she ever going to recognize the difference?

"How can I believe you?" she asked.

"Can I prove I've never slept with another woman?"

She found herself praying he could. She loved him. She loved him so much.

"No man can prove that," said Reed with a sad shake of his head. "But there's nobody on the planet who can prove I have. I swear to God I've been faithful to you. I love you, Elizabeth." His hands loosened on her arms, and he pulled her into a hug.

Tears dampened her cheeks. "I'm so afraid."

He stroked his palm over her hair. "I'll keep you safe."

"I'm afraid of you, afraid of us, afraid that we're just not going to make it. I *want* to believe you, Reed. I *so* want to believe you."

He pulled back and cupped her face. "What's wrong, sweetheart? What's really going on?"

"I feel like I don't even know you anymore."

He looked puzzled. "You know me better than anyone."

"And you don't know me." She gave a strangled laugh. "Not that there's much to know. I'm nothing. I'm fading."

His tone was heartfelt as he searched her eyes. "You're everything to me."

"But I need to be everything to me. I need to have my own life, my own identity."

His voice went flat then. "So it'll be easier to leave me?"

"Do *you* want to leave *me?*" she asked.

"Never."

But there was still the gorgeous blonde, and there was still the scent of coconut embedded in her brain. "Now would be the time to tell me," she continued. "I won't hold it against—"

"*Never,*" he repeated.

She tried to trust him, tried with all her heart and soul to trust him, but it wouldn't quite come.

"Let's go away," he suggested. "Just you and me. We'll take a trip. We'll reconnect. We'll make love anytime, anywhere, as often as we want. Forget the stupid thermometer."

It was a tempting offer.

Away from New York, she'd have him all to herself.

And if he was having an affair, would he be so willing to leave? Maybe, just maybe, there was hope after all.

"We've already blown this month anyway," she ventured, half to herself.

He smiled. His expression relaxed, and when she looked deep enough into his eyes, she caught a glimpse of the man she'd first fallen in love with.

"Paris," he said, dipping forward. "Or Marseille. We'll rent a chateau and lock out the world."

His lips met hers in a familiar kiss. Her body quickened, and she longed to wrap her arms around him and bury her fears in his strength.

But she couldn't let herself do that. Not this soon. And not this time. They had things to work through besides lovemaking.

She drew back. "Are you serious?"

"Absolutely. I'll book the jet."

Reed had found a chateau for rent in the little town of Biarritz in southern France. It overlooked the craggy beaches, bleached castles and stone walkways of the Atlantic coast. They had their choice of ten bedrooms, the chef came highly recommended and, best of all, there wasn't a blackmailer or SEC investigator within four thousand miles.

He watched while Elizabeth gazed around the arched great room, taking in the bank of French doors and paned windows that revealed a stone veranda. The veranda overlooked the harbor, where waves crashed against the rocks and seagulls called on the afternoon breeze.

It was a cool day, but tourists and residents still dotted

the beach walk. And a few intrepid souls reclined on colorful towels on the sun-warmed sand.

"It's stunning," she said, turning in a circle to view carved wall panels, antique furnishings, rich draperies and crystal chandeliers hanging from twenty-foot ceilings.

After a minute, she grew still, facing him. A wariness shadowed the joy in her eyes.

There was definitely some work to do on their relationship. He wasn't exactly sure where to begin. Elizabeth had misunderstood the blonde hanging all over him at Alexander's. And, he admitted, he could see how that could have happened.

But it was obviously a misunderstanding, easily explained away. And he wasn't sure what he'd done to warrant her suspicion in the first place. Every step he took in life was designed to protect her, to make her life easier and happier. But, for some reason, that wasn't enough.

From what he could tell, this had all started with her crazy idea to get a job. Although why a woman with an unlimited bank account would need a job, he couldn't figure out. Was she bored? Lonely?

He would love to spend more time with her. He'd also love to give her a baby. And he was doing the very best he could on both of those fronts. But he couldn't force a pregnancy, and that unlimited bank account didn't magically regenerate itself. And, lately, the world seemed to throw down challenges as fast as he could rise to meet them.

He felt frustration building within him, but he couldn't give in to the luxury of that emotion. For some reason,

Elizabeth was unhappy. And, as her husband, it was up to him to fix the problem—whether it made any sense or not.

"Are you tired?" he asked gently. "Would you like to take a nap?"

"Could we walk instead?" she asked, turning her attention back to the windows. "Along the shore?"

"Of course," he agreed easily.

She smiled at that, and the frustration eased inside him.

While Elizabeth went upstairs to change into comfortable shoes and a sweater, Reed consulted with the chef on the menu. Jean-Louis also showed Reed a romantic, little dining alcove on the second floor. With a view of the lighthouse and the yachts in the harbor, it would be a perfect location for dinner.

When Elizabeth returned, Reed took her hand, leading her through the wide turret that was the foyer and out to the porch, down a cobblestone path and a short staircase to the beach walkway.

She turned in circles, gazing at the rolling waves and the rock promontories. "This is absolutely gorgeous."

"I think the town center is that way." Reed pointed south to the vintage, stone buildings and the international hotels.

"Let's check it out." Her hand tightened on his as they started to walk.

As they passed other tourists, she asked, "Did you know we have ten bedrooms in the chateau?"

"You counted?"

"I counted."

"It was hard to find a place on short notice." His travel agent had given them a choice of very high end or very low end. High end easily won.

"It seems like we should invite some friends to join us."

"Not a chance." This was their getaway. Theirs and theirs alone.

They came upon a shop with merchandise displayed on the stone sidewalk. Elizabeth ran her hand through a row of colorful silk scarves.

"Would you like one?" he asked, eyeing a bright purple and blue design.

She chose a lemon yellow, so he bought them both.

The next shop sold beachwear.

Elizabeth sorted through a rack of sundresses. "I had the strangest conversation with Heather the other day."

"Uh-huh." Reed checked out a white bikini and matching wrap, wondering if he'd convince her to wear it.

"They know we're trying to get pregnant."

Reed switched his attention from the bikini to Elizabeth, surprised by the revelation. "Did you tell them?"

She shook her head. "Brandon said it was in my eyes when I looked at Lucas and in my voice when I talked about him."

Reed nodded, his happiness dimming a notch. Suddenly, the scarves in the little bag seemed frivolous and inconsequential.

He took her hand and they moved on together in silence.

"Heather..." said Elizabeth, shifting tight against him as they maneuvered around a family of four. Then she took a deep breath and eased away. "Heather offered to be a surrogate mother."

Reed stopped in the middle of the walkway, and his chest contracted painfully. Did Elizabeth know something he didn't? Had there been bad news from Dr. Wendell? Was that what all this job and infidelity nonsense stemmed from?

"Why?" he demanded in a hoarse voice.

Elizabeth urged him to the edge of the path, out of the crowds, where a cliff dropped down to the crashing waves below.

"Were there more tests?" he probed. "Did you find out—" He couldn't voice the question.

"No more tests," she said quietly. "But it's been three years."

Reed braced his hands against the waist-high rock wall, clenching his fists and pressing his knuckles against the rough stone. Sure, it had been three years. But the first eighteen months or so, they weren't really trying for a baby, they simply weren't trying not to have a baby.

He'd assumed it would happen naturally. Thousands of women got pregnant every day of the year. Many of them weren't even trying; some were actively trying to prevent it.

And then there was him and Elizabeth, both with above-average intelligence, both healthy, both hardworking. Both of whom would be stellar parents. Yet they had to contend with charts and graphs and invasive tests, and still nothing happened. And now their family members were beginning to speculate.

"I *hate* this." He fixed his stare on the endless ocean. "It's none of Brandon's business. It's none of Heather's business. There are *way* too many people in our bed."

Elizabeth placed a hand on his tense forearm. "She was only trying to—"

"I don't care," Reed ground out. "I want it to stop. I want you and only *you*. I want it the way it used to be, with you purring and perspiring—"

"Reed."

"—arching and moaning—"

"Reed!" She pasted him with a censorious look, glancing meaningfully around at the families out shopping.

He swallowed. "I miss you."

"I miss you, too," she whispered, leaning against his arm, a sheen coming over her eyes.

"I don't want us to be self-conscious about making love."

"I know."

"My parents—" He stopped himself. Elizabeth didn't need to know his parents were also waiting with baited breath for any sign of pregnancy.

"They may not be crazy about my pedigree," she continued his train of thought. "But they definitely want you to procreate."

"My parents are snobs."

"You *think?*"

He chuckled at the tone of her voice, turning to brush a few stray hairs from her soft cheek.

Her skin was flushed, her smile wide, and the sunshine off the Atlantic highlighted her green eyes. "Can we talk some more about sweating and moaning?"

Arousal instantly hit him in the solar plexus. "Not here we can't."

"Back at the chateau? In one of our ten bedrooms?"

"I noticed the master bed was a four-poster," he pointed out, suddenly anxious to get her back there.

Her smile widened even further.

"And we have these new silk scarves." He waggled his eyebrows suggestively.

"I hope you're hinting that I should wear them."

He moved closer to rasp in her ear. "Among other, more interesting things."

"You've got to be joking."

"Why?" Lovemaking should be playful and fun.

With the heel of her hand, she playfully hit him in the shoulder. "You seriously want to tie me to the bed and have your way with me?"

"Absolutely." A sensual, compelling picture rose in his mind.

She coughed out an unintelligible protest.

"Trust me," he told her.

"Reed."

"Trust me." He pulled away and grasped her hand, urging her back along the walkway toward the chateau.

Seven

At the chateau, Jean-Louis was clearly delighted to see them. And when Elizabeth saw the beautiful table he'd prepared, and inhaled the luscious scents wafting from the kitchen, she knew making love would have to be postponed. She excused herself to change, finding her clothes freshened and hanging in the closet of the master bedroom.

She changed into a black cocktail dress then met Reed at the bottom of the formal staircase.

He gallantly held out an arm. "Would you care to accompany me to the wine cellar?"

She grinned to herself, feeling sexy and playful for the first time in months. "Can I trust you in the wine cellar?"

He grin broadened. "Come on down and find out."

She pretended to hesitate, but he turned them both into a short hallway that ended with a wood-plank door.

The stone staircase beyond it was narrow, and the light was dim. Reed kept a firm hold on her waist as they made their way to the bottom. There, he switched on an overhead light, and she drew in a surprised breath at the rows and rows of dusty wine bottles.

"We're looking for row eight." Reed led her down to the third rack.

"What are we looking for?" she asked.

"This," he announced, and his hands closed over her hips, lifting her to sit on a ancient, hewn-beam table in the middle of the aisle.

"What—"

He silenced her with a kiss, moving between her knees and wrapping his arms tightly around her.

His lips were cool and soft, moist and parted. His tongue gently explored the recesses of her mouth, and she felt shards of arousal work their way out from the pit of her stomach to the tips of her fingers and toes.

His hands moved to her bare knees. His kisses explored her neck, her ears, her shoulders, while she gripped his upper arms for support.

His fingertips circled higher on her thighs, leaving a burning trail of want behind them.

"I had a feeling I couldn't trust you down here," she breathed.

"You can trust me completely." But his fingers hooked around her panties, tugging them down.

She gasped and grasped his forearms. "Not here." She glanced around at the cold, dusty room.

He chuckled. "No. Not here." But he pulled her panties to her ankles, peeling them off over her heels. Then he tucked them firmly into his inside pocket.

He gazed hotly into her eyes. "Later."

"But—"

He silenced her with a finger across her lips. "We're on vacation, Elizabeth. We can play."

He lifted her down from the table, smoothing her skirt back into place. Arm still around her, he guided her toward the narrow staircase.

"Reed?"

"Yes?"

She tipped her head to look back at him. "The wine?"

"Right."

Elizabeth leaned back against the solid table, content to let Reed choose the year and the winery. If there was anything her well-bred husband knew, it was good wine.

She watched the play of his muscles as he reached into the bins, considering and returning bottles. She shifted down the table to bring his profile into view. There was no doubt he was a gorgeous man, and a slow pulse of sexual arousal remained steady in her bloodstream while the cool air circulated around her bare legs.

She couldn't help but picture the big, four-poster bed. The silk scarves also tickled their way into her imagination, making her shiver. She and Reed had more complex problems than a long night of pleasure could solve, but reconnecting sexually wouldn't hurt. It might even help. And it could definitely be satisfying.

"After you," he said, gesturing to the staircase with one of the bottles he'd chosen.

They made their way back to the second floor, where a young French woman assisted Jean-Louis in serving them an artichoke and baby greens salad. It was followed by pumpkin soup, bay shrimps, salmon, a cheese tray, and finally the most heavenly torte she'd ever tasted.

By the time the final dishes were cleared away, Elizabeth had kicked off her shoes and curled up in the rich, velvet upholstery of the big, Louis XV chair.

"Come here," Reed rumbled, a half smile on his face and heat smoldering deep in his midnight-blue eyes.

Elizabeth's sexual arousal returned in a rush. She set down her coffee cup, uncurled her legs and padded the length of the table to Reed's chair.

He took her hand, drawing her down into his lap. Pulling back her loose hair, he feathered soft kisses into the crook of her neck.

Footsteps sounded in the doorway, and she stiffened at the sight of Jean-Louis.

Reed's hand closed around Elizabeth's wrist, keeping her from jumping off his lap.

"We won't require anything further tonight," he told the chef.

"*Bonne nuit, monsieur,*" intoned Jean-Louis with a respectful nod.

"Oh, it will be," Reed whispered to Elizabeth as the door closed behind the chef.

"That was embarrassing," said Elizabeth.

"Exhibitionism not one of your fantasies?"

She drew back in astonishment. Sexual fantasies were definitely not a subject of discussion in their marriage. "No."

He chuckled and resumed kissing, his spread fingers delving into her hair. "Noted."

"Seriously, Reed. I'm not—"

"Noted," he repeated. "I'm not going to forget."

"But—"

He anchored her head and kissed her deeply on the mouth. His other hand stroked behind her knee, teasing its way up her thigh, reminding her she was naked under the little black dress.

Her arms snaked around his neck, and she breathed his name, leaning into another deep kiss, reveling in the play of his lips and tongue on her swollen mouth.

Her breasts rubbed against his broad chest, nipples coming erect, growing sensitized against the fabric of her clothes. Her skin began to tingle, itching, aching to be touched.

His hand cupped her bare bottom, sliding toward the small of her back, bringing the hem of her dress up to her hips. He began an intimate exploration, and perspiration soon slicked her skin.

She went for the buttons of his dress shirt, popping them from their holes, splaying her hands over his chest, starting an exploration of her own.

"I've missed you," he groaned.

She nodded, but words were beyond her capability right now. His skin was taut, his muscles firm, the fire in his veins transmitting itself to her very core.

His palm slipped back down her leg, covering her thigh, caressing her knee, exploring the curve of her calf, then teasing the arch of her foot. Her head dropped back, and his kisses found her neck. He made his way down her chest, while her hands moved to grip his shoulders, stabilizing her position.

He nudged her neckline, moving the fabric out of the way, kissing her nipples through the thin silk of her bra, leaving wet circles that cooled and puckered her skin unbearably.

A groan made its way up from her core, and his hand convulsed against her waistline.

"I love you," he whispered against her breast. "I am madly and passionately and completely in love with you."

"Oh, Reed."

"No matter what happens—" He pulled back, straightening, scooping her into his arms while her body throbbed with need. He carried her the length of the hallway, pushed open the master bedroom door, then closed it firmly behind them.

The lights were out, but the shine from the town and the glimmer of the lighthouse gave the room a luminous glow. Reed sat her on the edge of the bed. Then he stripped off his jacket and tie, his shirt still hanging open. He came down on one knee in front of her, parting her legs and easing between.

He hooked his fingertips into the top of her bra and tugged her forward. She came easily, kissing his mouth, running her fingers through his neat hair, shifting forward so that her dress bunched up and she came in contact with the bare skin of his abdomen.

He rolled her dress up over her head, unclipped her bra so that it fell between them. Then, his eyes boring into her body, he laid her back on the bed. He stroked his hand up the center of her belly, over her navel, between her breasts and across her shoulder.

His mouth followed the trail, leaving hot, moist spots along the way. Finally, he slid up beside her, lips coming down on hers, arms wrapping around her, pulling her solidly against the strength of his body.

His cotton shirt trailed over her skin, further sensitizing her belly, her breasts, her nipples. His hand circled down, touching her downy curls, lower still, until she gasped and arched off the bed.

His kiss deepened, and she convulsively dug her fingernails into his back. Her eyes closed. Her toes curled. Her thighs began to quiver, and her lungs struggled to keep up with her need for oxygen.

Then something brushed softly over her face.

She opened her eyes to see a yellow haze.

Reed stretched out her right arm, then trailed the scarf along it, wrapping the soft fabric loosely around her wrist.

He was joking.

He had to be joking.

But what an odd time to decide to be funny.

He moved her other arm, and she felt the same sensation along it. Something shivered deep down in her core.

"Reed?"

"Trust me," he whispered.

Then he rose, stripping off his shirt, his slacks and everything else.

She lay still, not moving her arms, not moving a thing, taking in every inch of his magnificent body as diffuse light played off the planes and angles of his muscles. His chest was broad, shoulders strong, arms toned, hands capable.

He leaned over her, and she swallowed.

Gripping her upper arms, he shifted her to the center of the bed, her head cocooning in the deep pillows. He placed one knee on either side of her stomach, without putting any weight on her.

He stretched her right arm out again.

He was not serious. He was *not*.

He wrapped the other end of the scarf around the bedpost.

She tried to talk, but her throat had gone dry, and the words turned into a rasp. She wasn't scared. She wasn't angry. In fact, she was sort of…

He stretched out the other arm.

"Reed," she tried, wiggling her hips.

He centered himself over her, capturing her gaze, looking directly into her eyes. "Do you think I'll hurt you?"

She shook her head.

"Do you think I'll do one single thing you won't like?"

She shook again. She wasn't scared. In fact, she was turned on. She was well and truly turned on at the thought of giving him free rein over her body.

"Do you trust me?"

She nodded.

He smiled. "Good."

Then he kissed her mouth. She opened wide, welcoming his tongue. Instinct told her to hug him, but she kept herself still instead.

He kissed her jawline, her neck and shoulders. He made his way to the tip of one breast, then drew the nipple into his hot mouth. She groaned, and arched, and he moved to the other. Sparks of hot sensation traveled the length of her body, flushing her skin, making her blood burn with need.

She hissed his name. But he took his time, indulging in her belly, her thighs, her knees, all the way to her ankles. On the way back up, he moved to the inside, closer, slower, until he hit the center, and she nearly arched off the bed.

Her breaths became pants, and her head thrashed from side to side. Her thighs moved apart, knees bending.

"Now, Reed," she finally cried.

He levered up on his arms, settling over her, pushing inside in one smooth stroke. And she gave a guttural groan. Her arms automatically went around him. The scarves fell away, and she realized he'd never tied a single knot.

She wrapped her ankles across the small of his back, trapping him to her, rising to meet him, reveling in the barrage of sensations she'd nearly forgotten could exist. Her need drove higher, her body grew hotter, as their slick bodies came together over and over again.

A roar grew in the depths of her brain, and a pulse at the base of her spine became insistent. It throbbed harder and faster, radiating out to engulf her limbs.

She moaned his name and tightened her body around him as his rhythm came harder and faster, until rockets exploded behind her eyes and warm honey seemed to fill every crevice of her body.

Then the pulse slowly subsided, and her limbs grew limp. Her legs fell down to the bed, and her lungs worked double-time to recover.

Reed smoothed her hair from her face.

"You're gorgeous," he said.

"I love you," she affirmed.

He pulled her tight, rolling them both, so she was cushioned by his body. Then he flipped a comforter over her back and tucked her head against his shoulder, stroking her hair, his chest rising and falling with his own deep breathing.

Their time in Biarritz was like a second honeymoon. As the days drifted by, Reed watched the tension ease from Elizabeth's expression. They walked the beaches, rented a yacht, tried windsurfing, and visited the funky little shops that dotted the town. They even bought and shipped home an oil painting of the local lighthouse.

They made love every night, most mornings, too. He felt like they were finally reacquainting themselves with each other's bodies. He dreaded going back to the fertility charts and programmed sex.

He was surreptitiously checking with Selina, Collin and Devon several times a day. He'd kept the communications quiet, not wanting to break the spell for Elizabeth. But he knew that issues were beginning to pile up on his desk, and their vacation had to come to an end.

Elizabeth resettled against him on a sofa in a little nook they'd found in the turret on the third floor of the chateau. The sofa faced a curved bank of windows that showed off the brilliant orange sunset over the ocean. A storm was forecast overnight, and Jean-Louis was reluctantly whipping up a gourmet pizza so they could dine casually.

Let it rain, and let the waves blow in. Reed was looking forward to a cozy evening with his fabulous wife. It was their last evening in France. Elizabeth didn't know it yet, but the jet was already on its way to the Biarritz airport.

"Why can't it always be like this?" she asked.

"Sunset?"

"I mean, us. Together. No worries, no problems."

Reed couldn't help but smile at her wistful voice. "Well, for one thing, we'd run out of money."

She straightened to look at him, curling her legs beneath her in slim jeans and a loose, sea-green sweater. "Would we?"

"Of course."

"Maybe we could sell off a few companies. Or maybe you could hire a manager to run them?"

"It doesn't work that way." Everything in his conglomerate was interconnected. It was also interconnected with his father's companies. Wellington International as a whole was worth a lot more than the sum of its parts.

"Then, how does it work?" she asked.

Reed wasn't sure how to explain the complexities of his job.

"The companies depend on each other," he told her. "And someone needs to watch out for the big picture."

"What about Collin?"

"Collin has his own job. He can't do mine, too."

She harrumphed out a sigh. "I think you're getting too puffed up with your own importance. They didn't miss you this week."

"A week's not very long." And he'd been monitoring quite a number of things via his laptop and cell phone.

"I like spending time together," she said.

"I like spending time together, too."

There was a light rap on the door. "Mr. Wellington?"

"Yes?"

The solid door creaked open, revealing one of the housemen. "A phone call for you, sir."

"Obviously something important," Elizabeth sassed.

"Obviously," he agreed, giving her shoulder a quick rub before getting up from the sofa. He was keeping his cell phone turned off most of the time, and he'd asked the office not to contact him through the chateau unless there was an emergency.

This better be good.

The uniformed man pointed to a telephone in the corner of the room, and Reed perched himself on a tiny, French provincial chair.

"Hello?"

"Reed, it's Mervin Alrick calling."

Reed was shocked to hear Elizabeth's father's voice. "Mr. Alrick?"

Elizabeth swiveled her head to look at Reed, brows knitting together in a question.

Reed shrugged in answer.

"I'm afraid—" Mervin cleared his throat. "I'm afraid I'm calling to give you some terrible news."

Reed's chest tightened in dread, his thoughts going to Elizabeth's mother. "Yes?" he asked slowly.

Elizabeth leaned forward, cocking her head, a look of concern growing on her face.

"It's Brandon."

"Brandon?"

Elizabeth came to her feet.

"Brandon and Heather were in a car accident on the coast."

"Are they okay?" Reed reached for Elizabeth, and she moved forward to take his hand.

"What?" she whispered.

Reed gave his head a little shake, concentrating on the call.

"I'm afraid—" Mervin cleared his throat again.

"Mr. Alrick?"

"They've died."

Reed felt like he'd been sucker punched. *They?*

"Both of them." Mervin's voice broke, while Reed pulled Elizabeth against him.

Watching his expression, her eyes had gone wide with fear.

"You'll tell Elizabeth," Mervin rasped.

"Yes. Of course. We'll be there as soon as possible. And Lucas?"

"Is fine. He was with his babysitter."

"My jet's in France. We'll go straight to San Diego."

"Yes…well…" Mervin was clearly struggling for control.

"We'll call you soon." Reed disconnected.

"Reed?" Elizabeth's voice was paper dry.

He turned to face her, bracing one hand on each of her shoulders.

"Why do we have to go to—"

"It's Brandon," said Reed, hating what he was about to do to her. "He was killed in a car accident today."

Elizabeth shook her head in denial. "No. No. That doesn't make sense."

"Heather was killed, too."

Elizabeth took a step back, still shaking her head.

"I'm so sorry, sweetheart."

Brandon was her only sibling, and she'd adored him.

"It can't be," she whispered, even as her eyes welled up with tears.

Reed stepped forward and pulled her back into his arms. She struggled against both his touch and the cruel reality of the situation. "No. No. I can't believe it. I won't believe it."

"I need to get hold of Collin." Even as he rocked her, Reed reached for the phone. "He'll contact the jet and make arrangements."

Elizabeth let out a low, keening moan that nearly broke Reed's heart.

"We have to get to California," he told her firmly. "Lucas needs us."

She stilled, looking up. "Lucas?"

"Lucas is fine. He's with a babysitter. But we need to get to him."

She gave a jerky nod, tears flowing freely down her cheeks. Reed wrapped one arm firmly around her shoulders, and used the other hand to dial Collin.

Eight

Elizabeth moved through the next week in a state of shock, picking up Lucas, consoling her parents, attending the funeral in California.

Thankfully, Reed handled the legalities of the will. While her brother had named her as Lucas's guardian, he had named Reed executor of the estate. Between Reed and Collin, she needed only to sign papers and direct the packing up of Lucas's things.

She briefly met with Heather's parents after the funeral. They were nearly paralyzed with grief. They barely spoke, but held Lucas as long as possible, clearly struggling with the fact he was moving to New York.

Finally, she was back in the penthouse. Lucas's nursery was set up and decorated, and he was settling into a routine with Elizabeth. He still seemed sad and confused at times, but started crawling around the apartment, pulling up on furniture and showing Elizabeth how many changes she'd have to make to protect both Lucas and their antiques.

After a while, when he curled up in her lap for his bottle or drifted off to sleep in her arms, she actually caught herself smiling. There was a permanent hole in her heart for her brother and sister-in-law, but Lucas needed her, and she'd do everything in her power to make sure he grew up loved and protected.

She kissed his silky hair, carefully shifting him to her shoulder to carry him to his crib. His nap was late today. He'd been restless and fussy, chewing on everything he could find. His cheeks were pinker than usual, and his bottom gum was swollen red.

The poor little thing was getting a tooth.

Elizabeth came carefully to her feet.

There was a knock at the door, and he had startled in her arms. She quickly cooed, praying he'd stay asleep.

Rena appeared from the kitchen, drying her hands on a towel.

Elizabeth signaled with a finger across her lips, and the housekeeper glided silently toward the front door, while Elizabeth trundled Lucas down the hall. She laid him carefully into the crib.

She left the bedroom door ajar and padded back down the living room. There, she found Rena with a courier envelope in her hands.

"It's for you." She handed it over.

The return address was for a California law firm. Elizabeth sighed. Some new will detail no doubt. The tears that were never far from the surface burned the backs of her eyes.

"I'll be in Reed's office." The envelope felt heavy in her hands. But it was better to get it over with.

She pulled the tab on the courier envelope as she walked into the office, releasing a thick sheaf of official-looking documents. There was a seal on the top sheet, and it was addressed to her.

She scanned the opening paragraph, frowned, went back and read it slowly.

As she read on, her heart all but stopped in her chest, and emotion squeezed her in a painful vise.

Heather's parents wanted Lucas. This was a legal notification that the Vances were contesting the will. They wanted Lucas back in California, wanted to raise him themselves, wanted to defy Brandon and Heather's wishes and rip Elizabeth's nephew from her home.

She galloped through the package, then reached for the telephone, her hand shaking as she dialed Reed's number. Unanswered, the call bounced to Devon's desk and Elizabeth asked for her husband.

"I, uh…" Devon hesitated. "He's out of the office."

"I'll try his cell."

But all she got was his voice mail. She left a message, as another knock sounded on the door.

"Mrs. Wellington?" Rena appeared in the office doorway. "Hanna Briggs to see you."

Elizabeth nodded. "Send her in."

Hanna was breezing into the office in seconds. "Baby asleep?" she asked. Her smile faded when she took in Elizabeth's expression.

"Take a look at this." Elizabeth shoved the papers across the desk.

With a puzzled frown, Hanna scanned the papers. Then she looked up. "They can't do that."

"They're doing it. They think they'll be better parents than me."

"That's ridiculous."

"They claim they've seen Lucas every day of his life, that San Diego is a better place to raise a child, that Lucas knows them better. Add to that, they're experienced parents, where I—" Elizabeth's voice broke. "I'm only experienced in buying designer clothes and planning parties."

Hanna reached across for Elizabeth's hand. "That's crazy."

"They're not wrong. I do buy designer clothes and plan parties. And until last week, I hadn't changed a diaper in my life."

"Well, that's it then. Because, I'm sure a diaper changing contest will be the first thing the judge thinks of when determining custody."

"You know what I mean."

"I do. But you're getting ahead of yourself again."

Elizabeth understood Hanna's point. She'd gotten ahead of herself when she thought Reed was cheating, and when she thought Joe might be a criminal.

"I can't get hold of Reed," she said.

"He's probably in a meeting."

"He's always in a meeting."

Things had definitely been better between them physically since they returned from France. But she could feel them slowly slipping back into their old routine. Although nine-month-old Lucas kept her busy, she couldn't help but notice that Reed's evenings were filling up with business obligations.

"You should call Collin," Hanna suggested.

"You hate Collin."

"Only because he's a lawyer. But they do have their uses."

Elizabeth thought about that. Should she wait for Reed? Or should she get things rolling on her own? She did want to develop some independence.

Getting a job was out of the question for her now that Lucas had arrived. But that didn't mean she couldn't start standing on her own two feet.

The strength and self-assurance of the coconut woman had wedged itself firmly into Elizabeth's mind. For some reason, she knew deep down in her soul that Reed respected that kind of a woman.

"Collin it is."

When the line connected, she heard female laughter, then a voice that sounded vaguely like Reed's. Elizabeth's spirits lifted.

"This is Collin."

"It's Elizabeth calling."

"Oh. Hello, Elizabeth." The background sounds suddenly stopped. "How can I help you?"

"Are you by any chance with Reed?"

"Not at the moment. Do you need to get him a message?"

Too bad. "Actually, I need some legal advice."

There was a pause. "Sure."

"I received a notice today that my sister-in-law's

parents are contesting my brother's will." She gave him the details.

"Does Reed know about this?"

"I haven't been able to get hold of him."

"I'll have him call you." And the line went dead.

Elizabeth replaced the receiver and frowned at Hanna. "Not a lot of help." Then, remembering the opening to the conversation, she said, "It's funny. It almost sounded like—"

The phone rang on the desk. She grabbed it quickly. It was Reed.

She felt a rush of relief. "Did you get my message?"

"From Collin?"

"I thought you weren't with Collin."

"I'm not. He called me."

So Reed picked up the calls from Collin, but not the ones from her? "Where are you?" she asked.

"What's going on? Collin said the Vances contacted you."

Elizabeth explained the contents of the letter.

"Collin's going to come by and pick up the package," said Reed. "I don't want you to worry about it."

"How can I not worry about it?" She glanced at her watch, noting that it was nearly five. "Aren't you coming home now?"

"Not for a while. I've, uh, got a conference call with the West Coast."

"I see." Elizabeth didn't disbelieve Reed. Problem was, she didn't completely believe him, either. There was something in his tone that didn't quite ring true, something that made her feel he was searching for excuses.

She didn't like feeling this way. But the further they got from Biarritz, the more her confidence faded. If he loved her the way he said he did, shouldn't he be rushing home? Shouldn't Lucas and she be the most important things on his mind?

Reed hung up the phone and looked across the table at Collin. "Can you head for the penthouse and pick up those documents?"

Collin immediately rose. "You bet."

Reed cursed the fact that he couldn't leave right now. Elizabeth had too much on her plate. She was working round the clock to care for Lucas, while struggling to get over her brother's death.

Collin left the boardroom as Gage Lattimer walked in.

"What's up?" Gage took the chair across from Reed.

"This," said Reed, sliding his latest problem across the table. It was another letter from the blackmailer.

"Don't touch it," he warned Gage. If he hadn't obliterated them by opening it, the police might be able to raise fingerprints.

Gage read the short letter.

Hammond and Pysanski are the beginning. I'm the only one who can stop this now. Pay up!

When Gage looked up, his eyes were thunderous. "Who is this guy?"

Reed shook his head. "Trent stopped the Hammond and Pysanski connection from being reported in the media."

"Is it somebody close to you? Or somebody connected with the police?"

Reed had no idea. But this was a very disturbing turn of events. "If he's either of those things, you have to wonder how deep the frame-up goes."

"You think he could actually nail you?" Gage paused. "Or me? Why isn't he shaking me down?"

"Whoever did this has been thinking about it for a long time. Maybe he's planted evidence against me but not against you."

"I'm merely collateral damage?"

Reed coughed out a laugh. "Maybe. Or maybe he thinks I'm worth more money."

"You are."

"There you go."

"Ten million," mused Gage. "How long would it take you to raise that kind of cash?"

"Five minutes," said Reed honestly.

Gage nodded as Selina breezed into the room.

She reached into her briefcase, pulled out a plastic bag, and tweezered the letter safely inside. Then she sealed it, sat down and turned it so that she could read.

"I'll take this to a private lab. I doubt we'll get fingerprints. The operation has been too sophisticated so far to make a mistake like that."

"What about the police?" Reed asked her.

"I'm not putting this into the bowels of their backed-up crime lab. I'll get to them later."

"Any more clues? Anything else at all to go on?"

"I'm still following up on Hammond and Pysanski. In my opinion, we have a better chance of clearing up the SEC thing than finding the blackmailer. It we cut the SEC investigation off at the knees…" She snapped her fingers in the air. "Poof, the blackmail problem is gone."

"For me, anyway," said Reed. The blackmailer undoubtedly had other victims in mind.

"And, since you're the one paying my salary, you're the one I care most about."

"And me?" Gage put in, in a voice tinged with mock offense.

"You'll be a collateral victory," said Selina.

"You heard me say that?" asked Gage.

"I hear everything." She gave her attention back to Reed. "Something triggered this second letter. We're going to have to go over the details of your past few days."

Reed nodded in resignation, desperately worried about Elizabeth, and hoping Collin was taking good care of the will issue. Lately, it seemed as if Reed were being dragged simultaneously in a dozen different, yet crucial directions.

Elizabeth sat in the wingback chair opposite Collin.

"On my preliminary read," he was saying, the legal documents in his hands, "I'm feeling very optimistic. But I have a friend who's a member of the bar in California. I can get him to fly out tomorrow so that we can start on a proper plan of defense."

Elizabeth nodded, grateful to Collin. He was cool and controlled, and his expertise shone through at every turn in the conversation. But she couldn't help thinking that Reed should be here instead. It should be her husband who was offering comfort and advice, not his lawyer.

Then she berated herself for that train of thought. Hanna was right. Elizabeth needed to stand on her own two feet.

"I'd like to meet with your friend," she told Collin, squaring her shoulders. "I'm available anytime."

"I'll set it up."

The penthouse door opened, and they both turned to see Reed stride in. "What did I miss?" he asked.

Elizabeth glanced at her watch. It was nearly nine.

"I read the package," said Collin, coming to his feet. "I'm going to ask Ned Landers to fly in tomorrow."

Elizabeth stood to face Reed. "It's all under control. You don't need to worry."

Reed drew back sharply. "That's—"

"I know you're busy," she put in. Then she turned and reached out to shake Collin's hand. "Thank you very much for your advice, Collin. I appreciate your taking the time."

"Not a problem," he answered. "I'm always available for you, Elizabeth."

At the other side of the room, Reed stayed silent.

"Good night," Collin said to them both.

As soon as the door shut behind Collin, Reed turned on Elizabeth. "What the hell was that all about?"

She blinked at him in surprise. "What?"

"'I don't need your help, Reed,'" he simpered. "'It's all under control.'"

"It *is* all under control. Collin says we're in a very strong position. He says the Vances would essentially have to prove we're unfit parents to win in court."

"It's nice to know what Collin had to say, but what about what *I* have to say?"

"You weren't here."

"I had a meeting."

"You *always* have a meeting." She cringed at the sarcasm in her voice.

Reed's tone grew stronger. "I would have been here if I could."

"Keep your voice down."

He drew an exasperated breath. "I want the details."

She pointed to the papers on the round table. "Help yourself."

"I also want to know exactly what Collin said," he warned, scooping up the paperwork.

"I'll tell you everything I remember."

His eyes narrowed, and he peered at her.

"What on earth is the matter?" she demanded.

He was acting as though he were jealous of Collin.

Reed was stonily silent for a long beat. "I don't like being replaced by my lawyer. This is *our* problem, not your problem alone."

"I can take care of it, Reed. I'll have professional help."

His complexion turned ruddy. "So, you don't need me? Is that what you're saying?"

"Isn't that exactly what you said to me?" Even as she lobbed the volley, Elizabeth silently acknowledged that she didn't want to have this fight. Lucas was what mattered. All of her energy and emotional resources needed to be directed at him for the time being.

Reed turned sharply, and marched down the hall into his office.

Now she'd done it. The closeness they'd shared in France was officially a distant memory, and the cool formality from before their trip had turned to hurt and anger. And it was her fault. Fawning over Collin's presence had been a passive-aggressive slam at Reed's absence.

She screwed up her courage and followed him down the hall, carefully sliding open the door.

"Reed?" she ventured.

Without looking up, he grunted an acknowledgment.

"I'm sorry."

That got his attention.

"We should work on this together," she said calmly. "And I do appreciate your perspective."

"He's my son, too, you know."

Her eyes clouded, and she blinked rapidly. "Of course. I thought you were too busy. I was trying…"

Reed let the sheaf of papers flatten on the desk. "I'm sorry I was late." His jaw tightened. "Things are complicated…at the office right now."

She nodded, even though she didn't understand what he meant. But then she never had been privy to the intricacies and machinations of Wellington International. "Lucas is what matters."

"Yes, he is. We're his parents now, Elizabeth, and we need to ensure his well-being. On all fronts."

A tear slipped down her cheek. "Why are they doing this?"

Reed shook his head. "Grief over Heather? Maybe a desire to cling to a little piece of her?"

"But Brandon and Heather chose *us*." Elizabeth didn't know the Vances. They could be selfish or mean-spirited, they might even be fanatical about something. There was a reason her brother and sister-in-law had entrusted Lucas to her care, and she wasn't going to let them down.

"And the court will see it that way," said Reed. "We'll talk to Ned Landers together."

"Together," Elizabeth agreed. But a little part of her couldn't help wondering if Reed would make the meeting.

Nine

Ned Landers advised Reed and Elizabeth to carry on with their ordinary lives. The only leg the Vances might have to stand on is if they could paint Reed and Elizabeth as unsuitable parents. That task would be all but impossible.

Although Elizabeth had been focused on Lucas, her party planner and neighbor, Amanda Crawford, had carried on with the anniversary party plans. Ned recommended that they go ahead with the party. It sent a signal that their marriage was strong, and that they had a good support network of friends and extended family, helping to paint them as a stable family unit.

Hanna had volunteered to babysit Lucas for the

evening, insisting that she was the only one he trusted and that she hated big parties anyway. Elizabeth knew that was true, so she went along with the plan. For some reason, Reed had also insisted Joe Germain spend the evening in the penthouse.

Hanna had protested the arrangement. That is, until Joe showed up at the door and she got a good look at the tall, übermasculine man.

Elizabeth supposed Joe was a handsome man, in a caveman kind of way. Although, if a woman were turned on by physical power, Joe was about as good a fantasy as a girl could get.

Judging by Hanna's speechless, wide-eyed stare, she had a thing for physical power.

"Thanks for coming, Joe," said Reed, appearing from the kitchen.

Joe headed for Reed, giving Hanna a curious nod of greeting as he passed.

Hanna's gaze locked on the rear view of Joe.

Elizabeth elbowed her friend. "Down, girl. I don't think he's allowed to make out on duty."

"How would you know?"

"It must be in the handbook or something."

Hanna grinned. Then her gaze drifted up and down Elizabeth's red satin evening gown.

"You're going to knock 'em dead," said Hanna. "I wish I had your clothing budget."

"I feel pretty spoiled tonight," Elizabeth admitted. Reed had insisted that her gown be custom-made and dramatic.

Hanna gathered Lucas from Elizabeth's arms.

"There are a couple of bottles for him in the refrigerator," said Elizabeth, smoothing his hair and kissing his chubby baby cheek as she ran down the instructions.

"Yes, Mommy," Hanna sing-songed, and Elizabeth's thoughts went immediately to Heather.

"Sorry," Hanna whispered.

"It's all right. We have to move forward. And I guess I'm the one to do it."

"You're doing beautifully," said Hanna.

Elizabeth took a breath, and Reed appeared at her side. "Ready?" he asked.

"I don't know how regular parents do this," said Elizabeth, reluctant to leave little Lucas.

Joe stepped up. "I'm trained in fire safety, first aid, defensive driving and, well, hand-to-hand combat."

Reed grinned. "See that? We have absolutely nothing to worry about."

"Do you change diapers?" asked Hanna, obviously trying for a joke, but her voice came out breathy.

"Whatever's necessary," Joe said easily, lifting Lucas with a deft gentleness out of Hanna's arms and tucking him against his shoulder like he'd been doing it all his life.

Elizabeth wasn't sure, but she thought Hanna might have fallen instantly for Joe.

Reed held out an arm to Elizabeth. "Shall we?"

She smiled up at him, determined to enjoy her evening. She linked her arm into his as they turned for the door.

"Is Joe single?" she whispered under her breath.

"I think so. Why?"

Elizabeth glanced back at Hanna's expression. Her friend looked liked she'd been dropped straight into her deepest fantasy.

* * *

It wasn't often that Reed imagined himself in a science fiction story. But, at the moment, he would take it very kindly if somebody would please *beam him up*.

"I understand that these things can happen," continued Vivian Vannick-Smythe, a halo of feathers that served as a hat quivering around her lined face while she gesticulated her story. "And I'm certainly not one to stand in judgment."

Reed choked back a laugh at that statement.

While Vivian carried on about the SEC investigation and how it was all about her, he scanned the crowd for Elizabeth, wondering why, since this was their anniversary party, he'd spent so little time with her. Then he saw her dancing with Prince Sebastian. The man was holding her too close for Reed's taste. If not for the Prince's European sensibilities and the fact that he was getting married in Caspia on New Year's Day to his American assistant, Tessa Banks, Reed would have had words with the man.

"I think the reputation of the entire building is at stake," Vivian prattled on. "And if I were you—"

"You're not me," Reed pointed out.

Vivian took an imperious breath, the feathers jiggling again. "If I were you, I would do everything in my power to bring a speedy end to this embarrassing episode."

"You don't think I'm already doing that?" he asked.

Her eyes narrowed. "You should think long and hard about how you go about protecting your family, your friends and your neighbors…."

Reed drew back from her shrewd expression and the odd turn of phrase.

"From the crushing embarrassment of being associated with an accused criminal," she finished.

"Right," said Reed. "The crushing embarrassment of my neighbors is my primary concern at the moment."

"Good evening, Reed," came a familiar male voice.

Vivian's head came up, her self-confidence instantly evaporating.

"Good evening, Father," said Reed.

Anton stared Vivian down until she mumbled something unintelligible and scooted away.

Reed resisted the urge to thank his father.

"Elizabeth is looking well."

Reed turned his attention to the dance floor, agreeing that his wife looked incredibly beautiful, particularly considering everything she'd been through. "She's coping the best she can."

"I understand she's taking care of her nephew now?"

"Our nephew," Reed corrected.

"Yes, of course. And there are some grandparents in the picture?"

Reed gazed at his father's inscrutable expression. "You mean the Vances?"

"I understand they'd like to raise the boy."

"Lucas. His name is Lucas. And we're his legal guardians."

"Do you think that's wise?"

An uncomfortable feeling wedged its way into Reed's stomach. "It's not a matter of wise or unwise, Lucas *is* our responsibility now."

"Unless the grandparents win the court case."

"They won't."

His father squared his shoulders and set his jaw. "I wonder if you've thought this through."

Reed waited to see where Anton was going.

"Have you considered the impact this...nephew—"

"Lucas."

"—will have on your future children?"

And then Reed got it. And it was horrible. "Please tell me you're not suggesting—"

"He's not your natural-born son."

Reed coughed out a hollow, disgusted laugh. "You're worried about his pedigree? You're worried that he will somehow detract from...what? Their inheritance? Will his bad breeding somehow rub off on them?"

Anton's eyes turned to flints and he put his infamous intimidation mask in place. But it wasn't about to work on Reed.

"I'm adopting Lucas," Reed said firmly. "He'll have every legal right of any other child I may or may not have in the future."

The mask slipped. "He'd be your eldest son. The Wellington heir."

"Yeah," said Reed. "How about that."

"I can't let you—"

"There is nothing, *nothing* you can do to stop me." He leaned in, making his point loud and clear. "And, believe me when I tell you, it is not in your best interest to try."

Then he turned and walked away.

"Reed?" Collin appeared by his side, falling into step.

"Where's the nearest bar?"

Collin pointed to one corner of the ballroom, and Reed started in that direction.

"You okay?"

"Fine," said Reed, forcing himself to switch gears. His father was his father, and there was nothing he could do to change that. He could only protect his family as best he could from the man's interference.

"What's up?" he asked Collin.

"They've set a court date in California," Collin told him. "In three weeks."

Reed digested the new information as he ordered their drinks. "What are Ned Landers's thoughts?"

"He's somewhat worried about the Vances' existing relationship with Lucas. They have documentary and pictorial evidence of having seen him nearly every day. They set up a scholarship trust fund for him mere days after his birth—"

"I could set up a scholarship trust fund," said Reed. Trust fund, hell. He was about to make Lucas a boy-king.

"Too little, too late," said Collin as they moved to a quieter spot with their drinks. "Besides, our argument isn't that you've been close to Lucas since his birth, it's that you and Elizabeth were Brandon and Heather's choice as guardians. Economic wherewithal is self-evident. You just need to keep your head down and your nose clean."

Reed knew what he meant. The SEC investigation.

"Innocent until proven guilty," Reed pointed out. "Surely a judge understands that."

"They'll try to use it."

"Let 'em."

"Don't get hostile," Collin warned.

"I don't need to get hostile. I'm in the right."

"And don't get cocky. Some judges see wealth as a handicap, not an advantage."

"Because I'm rich, I'm de facto strange?"

"Something like that."

"That's bullshit."

"Hostile again," Collin warned.

"Maybe you should go to the hearing instead of me."

"You mean with you?"

"I mean instead of me." The night the legal papers had arrived bloomed in Reed's mind, surprising him with the rush of anger it provoked. "You did a good job taking my place with my wife on Wednesday."

Collin stood stock-still, his martini halfway to his lips. "Don't be an ass."

"Elizabeth seemed pretty grateful."

"You sent me," Collin pointed out.

"We both know why I wasn't there."

"You accusing me of something?"

Reed squared his shoulders. "Is there something to accuse?"

Collin nodded to Reed's drink. "How many of those have you had?"

"Not nearly enough."

"You actually think I'm putting the moves on your wife?"

The blunt question stopped Reed in his tracks. "No." Of course not. The very idea was ridiculous.

"Good. Because if I want your wife I'll tell you straight up. Then we'll duke it out."

"Seems fair," said Reed with a shrug, acknowledging that his anger with Collin was completely misdirected. "But I think I could probably have Joe kill you."

"True enough," Collin agreed easily. "But first, we have to deal with this court date."

"Yeah." Reed swirled the ice cube in his glass. "I don't know what the hell happens if that doesn't go our way."

"Odds are with us on that one." Then Collin nodded to the foyer. "Wish I could say the same thing about the SEC investigation."

Reed followed Collin's line of sight, catching Selina hovering in the archway. Her jaw was compressed, and her eyes were hard.

"Damn," Reed muttered. He glanced to the dance floor where Elizabeth was in the arms of another lucky partner who wasn't Reed. "Tell me, when does this party get fun?"

"Want me to come with you?"

Reed shook his head, placing his empty glass on a nearby tray. "I want you to keep an eye on Elizabeth. Run interference if you need to."

"You got it," said Collin, moving off as Reed headed for Selina.

"What's going on?" he asked her, putting a hand on the small of her back and moving her to one side.

"It's Hammond and Pysanski." She sounded almost breathless.

"What about them?"

"There's evidence—dates, purchases and profits—that this isn't the first time one of Kendrick's committee decisions has netted them a windfall."

Reed glanced back into the ballroom, realizing for the first time that Kendrick and his wife hadn't shown up for the party. Had Reed underestimated the significance of this problem to Kendrick? Was it possible the senator was actually guilty?

Reed moved closer to Selina, lowering his voice. "Go on."

"Hammond put fifty thousand dollars into a company called End Tech in 2004. Two months later, the company won a federal contract for wireless R&D. Both Hammond and Pysanski bought into Norman Aviation right before a big helicopter award in '06. And, last year, Hammond went big on Saville Oil Sands just in time for the stock split."

Reed swore.

"Yeah," Selina agreed. "Add that to Ellias, and you've got yourself one hell of a pattern to put in front of the jury."

"And Kendrick can be connected in each case?"

"His committee made the pivotal decision every time."

"I'm screwed," said Reed, gripping the back of his neck.

"You're innocent," Selina pointed out.

"Tell that to a jury of my peers, after the prosecution shows them pictures of my real estate holdings and my airplanes."

She glanced away. "Okay. It's a challenge all right."

It was the first time Reed had seen even a hint of anxiety in the woman's eyes.

He leaned in, wondering just how much of a problem this new evidence would be. "Selina?"

Her teeth came down on her lower lip, and she gazed at him with a frankness that said more clearly than words they were in big trouble.

Whirling in the arms of her neighbor, Trent Tanford, Elizabeth caught yet another glimpse of Reed in the foyer. He was in deep conversation with a woman she couldn't place. The woman wasn't dressed for the party, but wore a pair of jeans and a blazer. Elizabeth could only see the woman's back, but Reed's expression was intense.

He touched the small of the woman's back and moved her off to one side, out of Elizabeth's sight. The song ended, and Elizabeth quickly thanked Trent, crossing behind a marble pillar for a better look.

Several friends stopped her to chat, and she was briefly distracted by a glimpse of Amanda Crawford. The normally vivacious and bubbly woman looked upset. She was cloistered in a corner with a very pregnant Julia Rolland, and the two looked to be having an intense discussion.

But then Reed came back into view. He was still talking with the mystery woman. Elizabeth took a few more steps. Then, suddenly, the woman turned.

Elizabeth's stomach plummeted to the floor. For a second, her limbs were paralyzed and a roaring in her ears nearly drowned out the music.

It was the coconut woman.

Reed had stepped out of his own anniversary party to have an intimate conversation with the woman he'd lied about at work and brought into their home. What was going on?

What had he done?

"Elizabeth?"

She blinked a man into focus in front of her. Gage.

"Care to dance?" he asked, holding out a hand.

No. Elizabeth did not want to dance. She wanted to rant and rail, and scream at fate, scream at Reed, demand an explanation for what looked absolutely damning.

"Sure," she said instead, and let Gage's strong arms pull her into the rhythm of the music.

She tried to ignore Reed, but that was impossible. The conversation was still going on. Reed looked angry. Coconut woman looked upset. Then Collin joined the two of them. Collin, the traitor. Had he been routinely covering for Reed's trysts?

How long had this been going on? Had Biarritz been some kind of a trick?

"Uh, Gage, that woman in the foyer with Reed. Do you know her name?" Elizabeth was proud of how even she managed to keep her voice. "We met at Reed's office a few weeks back, but I'm embarrassed that her name's slipped my mind."

Gage hesitated long enough to make Elizabeth want to sock him. Was he in on it, too? Was there a conspiracy of silence among rich, powerful men? Did they all keep a mistress? Had she been hopelessly naive all these years?

"I think it's Selina."

Elizabeth waited, taking in the discomfort on Gage's face.

"She's connected to law enforcement somehow," he said.

Right. First Selina was a job applicant, then a client, now in law enforcement? Elizabeth wasn't stupid. This was a conspiracy, and she couldn't trust anyone.

"That sounds right," she said with a bright smile. She blinked, searching the room for something else to concentrate on while the song finished.

She spotted Amanda again. The woman still looked upset, but this time she was talking to Alex Harper. While Elizabeth watched, Alex touched Amanda on the shoulder. The woman's lips compressed. She turned away, and Alex's smile turned to a frown. It looked like he called her name, but she kept walking.

Then finally the dance ended. Elizabeth gave her husband one last fleeting glance then slipped out a side door.

"I didn't expect you this early." Hanna hopped up from the sofa as Elizabeth entered the penthouse.

"I missed Lucas," Elizabeth lied, hoping she'd successfully hid evidence of her crying jag while she was in the back of the limo. In case her eyes were still red, she busied herself hanging up her coat and putting her purse away.

"He was a doll," said Hanna. "And Joe really does change diapers."

"Pediatric protection detail," Joe put in, levering up out of his chair.

"But you were right," said Hanna in a breezy voice. "He's not allowed to make out while he's on duty."

Elizabeth sputtered out a laugh. "You propositioned my bodyguard?"

"I'm your driver," Joe corrected.

"He's a stickler for the rules," said Hanna with a saucy shimmy.

"Would you mind driving Hanna home?" Elizabeth asked Joe. The faster they left her alone, the faster she could fall apart.

"Not at all," he drawled. "There's a...little matter we need to finish."

"I..."

Elizabeth smiled, amazed that she could be happy for her friend when her own life was crashing down around her.

"Good night, Elizabeth," Joe offered as he propelled Hanna toward the door.

"I'll call you." Hanna waved.

"Lock up," he advised as he let the door swing shut.

Elizabeth turned the dead bolt and took two steps back. Then, she stopped, bracing a hand on the entry table and closing her eyes as the world spun around her. She felt genuinely dizzy.

What on earth did she do now?

The spinning stopped, and she walked into her home. She took in the furniture they'd had custom-made, the paintings she'd so lovingly chosen, the wrapped package leaning against the wall. It was the painting they'd purchased in France, when everything seemed like it would work out.

What was Reed thinking? How could he make such tender, passionate love to Elizabeth while coconut... Selina was waiting in New York?

She made her way down the hall, listened by Lucas's door, then turned into the office. There, she did something she'd never done before. She opened Reed's laptop and booted it up.

It took only three tries to guess his password and get into his e-mail. She scrolled through hundred of entries, until she came to the dates they'd been in France. Selina Marin, Selina Marin, Selina Marin. There were dozens of e-mails from her, and dozens of answers from Reed.

Elizabeth didn't have the heart to read any of the messages. The last faint hope that she'd somehow been mistaken was gone. Reed had a mistress, and Elizabeth's life was a lie.

Ten

Reed couldn't understand why Elizabeth had left the party. If she was worried about Lucas, she should have said something. As it was, he'd been left in the embarrassing predicament of having to make her excuses.

Unlocking the penthouse door, he found himself struggling for patience. "Elizabeth?" He kept his voice low, not wanting to disturb Lucas if he was asleep.

"Elizabeth?" he tried again, dropping his keys on the table. Her purse and coat were here, and Hanna and Joe had obviously left.

He started down the hall, glancing into the office, Lucas's room, then, finally, the master bedroom.

"There you are." He stopped short, seeing an open suitcase on the bed. "What's wrong?" Had there been some news? Was she going to California?

She didn't answer, didn't look at him. Her cheeks were streaked with tears, and there was a stiffness to her walk.

"Elizabeth?" He moved toward her, arms out, fear rising in his throat.

"Don't touch me!" she snapped, jerking back.

"What? What's wrong?"

"You know perfectly well what's wrong." She met his eyes for the first time, and he was floored by the anger he saw reflected in her depths.

"What?"

She yanked open a drawer. "Don't play dumb with me."

"I'm not *playing* anything. Why are you packing? Where are you going?" His heartbeat thickened in his chest. Something was terribly wrong.

"Selina Marin. Name mean anything to you?"

Uh-oh. Had she heard about the blackmail? Was she afraid for Lucas? "I didn't want to tell you," he began, "because—"

"You don't think I can guess why you kept it a secret?"

Well, yes, of course she could guess. "There were so many things going on. You had so much on your mind."

Elizabeth gave a hysterical little laugh, then pressed a shaking hand against her mouth. "You think I was too *busy* to hear about your mistress?"

For a split second Reed was too stunned to react. "My *what?*" His harsh shout woke Lucas, and the baby cried out.

Elizabeth immediately moved for the door.

Reed grabbed her by the arm. "What the hell are you talking about?" he thundered.

"Let me go."

He released her, and she darted to the nursery.

Reed followed. "I have no mistress," he hissed from behind.

Elizabeth picked up the crying baby, rocking him against her shoulder.

"Did you hear me?" Reed demanded.

Elizabeth turned as Lucas's sobs subsided. "You're caught, Reed."

"Caught doing what?"

"I know she's not a client. I know she's not a job applicant. I know your friends and your staff have been covering for you. You lie when you say you're in meetings—"

"I do *not* lie."

"Keep your voice down."

"I do not lie, Elizabeth. When I say I'm in meetings, I'm in meetings. I can't always share the subjects with you, but that's for your own good."

She harrumphed a sound of disbelief. "How long, Reed? How long have you been sleeping with Selina Marin?"

"Selina Marin is a private investigator."

"There we have it," said Elizabeth. "Career number four for the intrepid Ms. Marin."

"She is a private investigator. And I'm not sleeping with her."

"Prove it."

Reed almost laughed. Elizabeth was as bad as the SEC, asking him to prove something didn't happen?

"I saw the e-mails," said Elizabeth.

"What e-mails?"

"The e-mails from France. You wrote to the woman every damn day. How could…" Tears welled up in Elizabeth's eyes, and she turned away.

Reed dragged a hand through his hair, wondering how everything in his life could get so far off-track. He could see that Lucas's eyes were fluttering closed, so he backed out of the nursery, giving Elizabeth a chance to settle him again.

He waited in the hall, his mind ticking through possible scenarios that had led her down this path. He had to come clean about the blackmail. He realized that. But how on earth had she interpreted Selina's PI activities as an affair? Surely it took more than business e-mails to the woman for Reed to be tried and convicted.

Elizabeth exited the nursery, pulling the door partway closed.

Reed reached out to her. "Come and sit down."

She shook her head.

"Please? Something's gone so far wrong, and we're not going to work it out unless we talk."

"I don't want to be lied to."

"I'm not going to lie."

She gave a little laugh. "A liar telling me he's not going to lie. How could I possibly doubt the sincerity of that?"

"Elizabeth." Now she was frustrating him.

"I'm done, Reed. It's over."

"How did you see the e-mails?"

She looked momentarily stricken. "I hacked into your computer."

"The password wasn't there to keep you out."

"You e-mailed her from Biarritz every single day. While you… While we…"

Reed remembered full well what they'd done in Biarritz. "Did you read them?"

Elizabeth shook her head.

He reached for her hand, but she jerked away.

"I'm being blackmailed, Elizabeth."

"Because you're having an affair?"

Reed clamped his jaw and counted to ten. "Let's sit down."

She set her lips in a mulish line.

"Do you want to know the truth?"

She blinked rapidly. "I want to know the truth. I need to know the truth. Don't lie to me anymore. Please, Reed. I couldn't stand it."

His heart contracted, but this time when he reached for her hand, she let him take it. He led her to the living room, to the wingback chairs in the bay window where they'd be facing each other.

"I'm being blackmailed," he began. "Last month, I got a letter demanding ten million dollars or 'the world will learn the dirty secret of how the Wellingtons make their money.' I ignored it. Then the SEC investigation started, and we realized it was connected to the blackmail. We also realized that my blackmail could be connected with Trent and with Julia and—here's the biggest problem— the police can't rule out that Marie Endicott's death wasn't a murder and wasn't connected to the blackmails."

"And you didn't tell me?" Elizabeth's voice was small.

"I didn't want to worry you. You were trying to conceive."

"How could you not tell me?"

"There was nothing you could do."

"I could have given you moral support."

"Yeah. Right."

Her expression turned thunderous, and she started to stand.

"I meant, I'm man enough not to burden my wife with my problems."

"So you burdened Selina instead."

"Yes. And Collin and Trent and the New York State Police Department."

"But not me."

"Elizabeth."

"I'm not made of spun glass, Reed."

"We were trying to get pregnant. The party was taking a lot of your time. Then the SEC thing hit, and there was Lucas. And I didn't think you needed to know there could also be a murderer on the loose. Dr. Wendell specifically said no stress. A murderer is stress, no matter how you slice it."

"So you hired Joe."

"Selina hired Joe."

Elizabeth shook her head sadly. "Let me make sure I've got the picture. You're not sleeping with Selina."

Thank goodness she finally got that part right. "I'm *not* sleeping with Selina."

"You're sleeping with me."

"As often as humanly possible."

She didn't smile, and he regretted making the weak joke.

"With Selina, you're sharing your troubles, your fears, your aspirations and your secrets."

Reed wasn't sure how to respond to that.

"And while we were in France, you were tying me to the bedposts—"

"—I never really—"

"—while discussing the weighty matters of our personal lives, our marriage and our future with *her.*" Elizabeth's voice rose to a fever pitch. "You know what I think, Reed?"

He was afraid to ask.

"I think you're married to Selina and having a fling with me." She rocketed out of her chair.

He jumped up. "That is completely unfair. *Completely.*"

Elizabeth turned on him. "I bet you spend more hours in a day with her than with me. And is there anything about you she doesn't know? She's chasing down a murderer, so I bet you have to give her all the details."

"You're bastardizing—"

"Do you lie to her about where you are? Who you're with?"

"Will you please settle—"

"I don't just want to share your bed, Reed. I need more than the few minutes you can spare around your other obligations. I need more than the scraps of information you deem safe to share with me. I need *you,* Reed. I need to share your life."

"You are sharing my—"

"This *isn't* a marriage. You and I have none of the fundamental pieces that couples need to build a life together. Yeah, we're good in bed. You can completely push my buttons. I even liked the silk scarf thing. But I need more. I need all of you. I cannot, I *will* not play second fiddle to your 'professionals.'

"I'm going to finish packing, Reed. Then Lucas and I are leaving."

"No, you're not."

"Yes, we are. And you can't stop us."

"*I'm* leaving," Reed said in a low, firm growl. "It's nearly midnight. You are *not* going to drag a baby out of bed and cart him off to a hotel in the middle of the night. I'll leave. You two stay here."

He didn't wait for her answer, simply headed for the door and left the penthouse. He had no other option. If she'd made up her mind, she'd made up her mind. He'd been the best husband he knew how, and if that wasn't good enough, the only thing left to do was step aside.

Elizabeth had just settled Lucas in his baby swing when Hanna arrived at noon the next day. "All I can say," she purred as the door clicked shut behind her, "is that Joe Germain sure knows how to take care of a girl's body."

"Good night?" Elizabeth asked, feeling exhausted from her own sleepless hours of tossing and turning. She knew in her soul that things couldn't continue with Reed, but she missed him desperately, especially in their big bed.

When she thought about the fact that he'd never be there again, that his strong arms would never wrap around her, that she'd never feel the satisfying, naked weight of him on top of her ever again, she wanted to collapse in a heap and cry her eyes out.

Hanna, however, was smiling. "Joe is the sexiest, toughest, most inventive man on the planet."

Elizabeth tried for a smile. "I never would have put you two—" She swallowed. "I never would have—"

"Lizzy?" Hanna peered into her eyes, concern growing on her face. "What the hell?"

As Elizabeth felt a fresh rush of tears, Hanna helped her to the couch, sitting down next to her and curling up her jean-clad legs. "What happened? The Vances? Lucas?"

Elizabeth shook her head. Her throat was raw and her chest felt like it was being squeezed by a giant rubber band. "Reed," she managed.

"The SEC thing?"

"I don't understand."

Elizabeth forced her emotions under control. She had to stop this. It was what it was, and no amount of crying would change that. "Reed and I split up last night."

"He was *not* having an affair. I know this."

"He might as well have been. He won't share his life with me, Hanna. The man was being blackmailed for ten million dollars, and he never even mentioned it. But to her—" Elizabeth's voice shook. "With her, it's a dozen e-mails a day."

"Like online sex?"

"Like online life. To me, he lies, he evades, he protects. She gets his hopes, his fears, his dreams. I want that," she said, stabbing her thumb against her chest.

Hanna cocked her head. "But he's not sleeping with her."

"No."

"And he is sleeping with you?"

"Was."

"And there's no way to fix the other? I mean, now that you know about the blackmail…"

"There'll be something else. Something else he worries will upset me, things he needs to keep secret for my own good. He's got this unbelievable protective streak, and he absolutely refuses to treat me like an adult. I could help. I could have helped."

"With the blackmail threat?"

"Yes."

"Yes. Well, of course. Because with your extensive experience with criminal investigative techniques, and your training in hand-to-hand combat…"

"You sound like Joe."

"Have you tried to talk to Reed?"

"Until I'm blue in the face." But nothing convinced Reed to let her in. If she couldn't get in, she couldn't be his wife.

"Do you still love him?" Hanna asked softly.

The tears that had dried up threatened again. "It's not like an on/off switch."

"I'm telling you," Reed said, rising to his feet and raising his voice so that Collin would get the point. "It's over. I left her at her request."

"And I'm telling you," Collin replied, "it *can't* be over for three more weeks."

"It's not like I won't support her. She can have anything she wants."

"That's not the point, and you know it."

Reed did know it. He simply didn't want to accept it. "To make her happy, I have to stay away."

"To protect her, you have to go back." Collin dropped back down in the guest chair. "The judge will want to see an intact family. You want Elizabeth to keep Lucas? You put your ass back in that penthouse and keep it there until the court case is over."

"It doesn't work that way," said Reed, trying to imagine Elizabeth's reaction if he showed up at the front door. "You don't understand. You've never been married."

"I'm not giving you marital advice," said Collin. "I'm giving you legal advice. Sleep on the couch. Eat at restaurants. You work eighteen hours a day anyway. It's not like you'll have to see each other."

Collin's accusation came too close to one of Elizabeth's complaints for Reed's taste.

"I don't work eighteen hours a day."

Collin snorted. "How many times last month did you have business dinners?"

Reed scanned back in his mind. "A few."

"Seventeen, to be exact. Devon showed me your schedule."

"Seventeen?" Reed turned the number over in his brain. Add to that his Chamber of Commerce functions, the two nights he gave speeches, and a couple of business trips to Chicago, and it started to add up.

He tried to picture his last dinner with Elizabeth. They'd eaten together at the anniversary party, of course. But he'd dealt with a flurry of problems while she danced with other men.

"Let me make one thing perfectly clear," said Collin.

"I have absolutely no designs on your wife." He paused while Reed's eyes narrowed. "But I'm glad she did it. If I was her, I'd have left you a long time ago."

"Wellington International doesn't run itself," Reed pointed out. He didn't attend business dinners because he'd rather be there than at home. They were important. They were necessary. Particularly when you were dealing with out-of-town guests or other cultures, the social aspect could make or break a deal.

"Don't you think I know that?"

"So, what's your solution?"

"My solution is to stay single."

Reed dropped back into his chair. "Looks like I'm about to do the same thing."

"But not for three weeks."

"Right," Reed reluctantly agreed. For Elizabeth, for Lucas, he'd be a man about it. She was going to resist. But he'd make her understand it was for her own good.

The last person Elizabeth expected to knock on her front door was Reed. It was surreal for him not to use his key. Plus, she'd been picturing him in her mind for so many hours, it was almost a shock to see him in person. Frustratingly, her heart gave a little lift. She squelched it.

He made no move to come in.

"Sorry to disturb you," he said instead, sounding formal even for Reed.

"No problem," she managed. "Lucas just went down for a nap."

Reed nodded. "I…uh…"

Did he need something? His clothes? Elizabeth struggled for the right way to behave.

"Can we talk?" he asked, looking very serious.

Her heart did the little lift thing again. "Sure."

She stood to one side and motioned him in, telling herself that nothing had changed. She could not, would not let him sweet-talk her into trying again.

He walked through the doorway and dropped his keys in their usual spot on the table. There was something about the unconscious act that tightened her chest and clogged her throat.

"What did you want to talk about?" She knew her only hope was to get this visit over with quickly. The pain of having him here was too intense, and she knew she was in for a fresh crying jag after he left.

As long as she could make it that far…

She sat down at one end of the sofa.

"I've been talking to Collin," Reed began. "He thinks…well, for Lucas…" He paced to the bay window.

Her stomach hollowed out. Reed wasn't going to fight her for Lucas. Please God, not that.

He didn't meet her eyes. "For the sake of Lucas, and the court case, and to maximize our changes of defending ourselves against the Vances, we should stay together until custody is settled. Three weeks."

Elizabeth was speechless.

Reed, here? Them, together, but not?

Reed slowly turned to look at her. "Elizabeth?"

"I…" she tried. How could she do it? How could she possibly see him every day while she was trying to get over him? It would be horrible, painful, impossible.

"I can't," she managed, her voice cracking.

His jaw clenched. "I know. That's what I said to Collin."

So, Reed had already refused. That was good. They'd find another way. A way that didn't require her heart to be shredded for twenty-one long days.

His blue eyes turned flat with determination. "But we have to."

A small whimper escaped from her, and she shook her head.

He crossed back to her, coming down on one knee. "If we separate, it gives the Vances exactly what they need. Their lawyer will use it to destroy our case. It puts Lucas at risk, Elizabeth."

She closed her eyes, fear and despair roiling within her. She wanted to throw herself into Reed's arms. She wanted his soothing voice to assure her that everything would be okay.

But he couldn't. And he never would again. She was on her own this time, and she had to be strong for Lucas. Her nephew, and her brother's last wishes were all that mattered now.

"I'll sleep on the couch," Reed offered. Since they'd set up the nursery, there was no spare bedroom.

"I can sleep on the couch," she croaked out, realizing the words told him she'd given in. Not that there was a choice. Logic told her that Collin was right. How could they present the better environment for Lucas if they were in the middle of a divorce?

Reed was shaking his head. "You need your sleep. You have a baby to take care of."

"And you don't?" She found an ounce of strength

somewhere to argue with him. "You have a corporation to run, criminal charges to defend against, and a black-mailer on your trail."

Reed unexpectedly gave a dark chuckle. "We're fairly pathetic, aren't we?"

She frowned. It was way too soon for humor.

"Sorry." His hand moved toward her face. He was going to brush her hair from her cheek, like he'd done a thousand, maybe a million times before. But he checked himself just in time. "I'm going back to the office. I'll probably be late."

Elizabeth watched him leave. The door swung shut behind him. The silence closed in around her. And the horrible feeling that she had made a terrible mistake by leaving him pounded relentlessly through her brain.

She didn't move until Lucas cried from the nursery.

Then she dug deep and found a smile for the baby, changed him, gave him his bottle and a handful of dry cereal. Together they built a block tower on the living room floor and watched a cartoon movie.

Rena took weekends off, so Elizabeth cleaned up after Lucas. By the time she gave him a bath, tucked him in, did his small load of laundry, and made up his bottles for the morning, she was dead on her feet.

After changing into a nightgown she settled down with a comforter on the sofa. Despite Reed's protests, she would sleep out here. It was less lonely than the bed.

She stared at the city light pattern on the high ceiling, telling herself she'd had no choice but to separate from Reed. Sharing such a minuscule portion of his life was worse than sharing none of it at all.

When his key turned in the lock, she closed her eyes, pretending to sleep.

She knew the exact second he spotted her. His footsteps froze, and he took a sharp breath. Then he moved to the side of the sofa.

"Elizabeth?"

She didn't answer.

"I know you're awake."

How could he possibly know that?

She heard him crouch down beside her.

Astonishingly, there was a trace of humor in his voice. "When you're asleep, you snore."

Her eyes opened. "I do not."

"It's very quiet, and very ladylike, but you definitely snore."

"You are lying."

He gazed the length of her body under the comforter. "What are you doing, Elizabeth?"

"Sleeping."

"My wife's not sleeping on the couch."

She struggled up onto her elbows. "Well, you're way too tall. I barely fit."

They both stared at each other in defiance.

"We have to share the bed," he finally stated.

"We can't share the bed."

"It's a big bed. I'll stay on my side, you stay on yours."

She gave her head an adamant shake. "That's crazy."

"Is there anything about this situation that's *not* crazy?"

She couldn't come up with an immediate answer.

His arms swept under her shoulders and knees.

"Reed!"

He lifted her. "You need your sleep. I need mine. And there's only one way to get it." He started for the bedroom.

His arms felt too good around her. His body felt too good against her. She had to fight to keep from melting into his strength. Twenty feet, ten, five, finally.

He stopped at the edge of the bed. He didn't immediately put her down, but stared into her eyes for a long moment, making her want all the things she couldn't have.

"Sleep well," he finally murmured then laid her gently down on the comforter.

Within seconds, he'd disappeared into the en suite. The fan began to whirr, and the water drummed against the floor of the shower.

Elizabeth buried her head firmly in her pillow and sobbed in utter frustration.

Eleven

Elizabeth awoke to silence. She'd slept deeply, and it took her a second to figure out why she had a sick feeling in the pit of her stomach. But then she remembered. Reed was leaving, and the pain came flooding back in force.

Morning sunshine fought its way through the bedroom curtains, confusing her. Lucas usually woke her up by seven. *Lucas.* Her gaze flew to the bedside clock, and she discovered it was nearly ten.

What was the matter with Lucas?

She sprang out of bed and jogged down the hall in her wrinkled nightgown.

His crib was empty. Panic clawed at her throat. But then she heard it. The gurgling sound of his voice. And then Reed's voice.

"The trick," Reed intoned, "is to make sure your foundation is solid. That means we use the red blocks first."

Lucas cooed in apparent agreement.

Elizabeth made her way down the hall. She stood in the doorway for a minute, watching the colorful tower go up before Reed spotted her.

"Good morning," he said, no inflection in his voice.

"Why didn't you wake me?"

He usually headed into the office first thing.

"You were tired," he said, keeping his attention focused on Lucas and the blocks.

"I could have—"

"You were tired." There was a snap in his voice this time, and his annoyed gaze met hers.

She cleared her throat. "I can take it from here."

"No problem," he said. "I wasn't planning to go into the office today."

Elizabeth blinked, trying to make the words compute.

"I've invited my parents for dinner."

Raw panic hit her system. "You did what?" Anton and Jacqueline *here?* In the middle of this? Her gaze flew around the slightly messy room.

"I invited my parents for dinner," he repeated.

"Why?" she wailed. "Rena's off. Did you call a caterer?" She rushed toward the kitchen. Was the Alençon tablecloth ironed? Did they have fresh candles? What about a centerpiece?

"I told them we'd send out for pizza."

Elizabeth stopped in her tracks, turning to stare at Reed. "Is that supposed to be a joke?" She really wasn't in the mood.

"No joke. They want to meet Lucas."

"You are planning to serve Anton and Jacqueline Wellington take-out pizza?" They were the reigning king and queen of New York society.

"I did warn them."

"You can't do this. I'll be mortified. They'll think I'm the worst hostess in the world. They already don't like me." Not that it mattered. They weren't going to be her in-laws much longer.

Reed came to his feet. "You worry too much."

"No. I don't worry nearly enough."

"I'll grab a six-pack to go with it."

"You absolutely will not. I'll going down to Pinetta's to pick up some filets. Do we still have that black labeled merlot in the wine rack?" Where was her purse?

Reed grasped her arm to stop her. "You're in your nightgown."

Elizabeth glanced down. She took a breath. "I'll change first...of course."

"You're not changing." He gave his head a shake. "I mean, you're not rushing out for filets. I told them pizza, and we're serving pizza."

"Why are you doing this to me?" Was he punishing her for leaving him? She searched his expression. "Do you hate me that much?"

He instantly let go of her arm, his gaze fixing on the wall behind her. "I don't hate you, Elizabeth." He seemed to gather his thoughts. "You're busy. You're ex-hausted. And you're upset. I've chosen this moment to take a stand against my father. If he wants to visit Lucas on short notice, he can do so while noshing on take-out pizza and sipping a beer."

The fight went out of Elizabeth. "So this is about you and your father? Not about punishing me?"

Reed's eyes narrowed. "*Punishing* you?"

She swallowed. "For leaving you."

He stared down at her while Lucas clattered blocks in the background, and a muscle ticked to life near his temple. "I would never, *ever* do a single thing to harm you. You are my wife, and I will protect you until you force me to stop. Understand?"

Her chest tightened painfully, and Elizabeth felt teary all over again. "Yes," she whispered. "We can serve pizza."

Reed could tell that Elizabeth was nervous.

He'd relented and allowed Elizabeth to order a centerpiece and use a tablecloth. And he would admit that it was entertaining to watch his mother tackle a slice of pizza on Wedgewood China with sterling silverware. She had pronounced it delicious. Elizabeth obviously hadn't believed her.

She was still jumpy after dinner when his mother climbed onto the floor in her linen pantsuit to play with Lucas. Elizabeth rushed to her side when Lucas grabbed a handful of Jacqueline's silk blouse, aiming it toward his mouth.

Jacqueline calmly untangled Lucas's chubby fingers and gave him a toy, which he immediately stuck in his mouth. Jacqueline laughed, but Elizabeth didn't relax her vigil.

Reed handed his father a second glass of German beer and sat down in the other wingback chair.

"Your mother and I have been talking," Anton began, setting his tall glass down on the round table between them.

Reed braced himself. He let his gaze rest on sweet, adventurous Lucas and elegant, compassionate Elizabeth—both of whom he loved to distraction. Somehow, some way, he was going to protect them from his father's narrow-mindedness. Even if he had to send them to live in France.

Anton's voice went gruff. "I was out of line the other day."

Reed turned to stare at his father's stern profile. Anton was also fixating on the cluster of people on the carpet.

"Excuse me?"

"About Lucas," said Anton. Then he cleared his throat. "I was out of line to suggest that you shouldn't adopt him."

Reed couldn't believe his ears. "You've changed your mind?"

"As I said. Your mother and I were talking."

Reed's mother? His mother had actually changed his father's mind about something as significant as the heir to the Wellington dynasty? Reed looked at Jacqueline with new respect.

Anton lifted his glass from the table and took a sip. "The baby makes your mother happy."

"Lucas," Reed prompted.

"Lucas," Anton acknowledged.

"He makes Elizabeth happy, too," said Reed, wondering if he should take a page from Lucas. A sappy smile. A big hug. A clap of his hands. Maybe Reed had been trying too hard as a husband.

"You should go to California," said Anton.

Reed turned his attention back to his father. "To do what?"

"Talk to the Vances. They want something. Find out what it is."

"They want Lucas," said Reed.

Anton shook his head. "They say they want Lucas. You find out what they really want."

"You're not suggesting this is a shakedown." It was preposterous to suggest that the Vances would use Lucas to get money. They obviously loved him.

"Your mother tells me babies are wonderful. But she also tells me that once you've raised your own, you want grandchildren. You don't want to start over.

"The Vances want something." Anton nodded to Elizabeth and Lucas. "This is your family. You go find out what it's going to take to fix the problem."

Reed considered his father for a moment. "You get a lot of advice from Mother."

Anton shot him a censorious look, and Reed braced himself for the fallout. But then his father's expression unexpectedly softened. "Yes. Well. That's just the way it is. The jet's at JFK. I took the liberty of clearing the schedule for tomorrow."

It took Reed all of thirty seconds to realize that the Vances weren't looking for a bribe. They loved Lucas, and they only wanted what was best for their grandson. After finessing his way around the issue for a good thirty minutes, in desperation, Reed had decided to put all his cards on the table.

He told the Vances about his and Elizabeth's infertility, of the strain it had put on their marriage, of her deep love for her brother, and her passionate desire to adhere to Brandon and Heather's final wishes.

He didn't brag about his wealth, but he didn't downplay it, either. Lucas would live in the finest areas of New York. As he grew, he would have access to private schools, culture, travel, a thousand experiences that would enrich his life.

Then, lastly, he admitted the problems he and Elizabeth were facing in their marriage. But he pledged to the Vances that he was going to do everything in his power to keep his family intact. As the words poured out of him, he knew they were absolutely true. He was going to fight tooth and nail for Elizabeth. He loved her, and he would find a way to win her back.

Margarite Vance cracked first. She admitted her deep fear that Reed would take Lucas away from them. Unlike Reed, they weren't wealthy, and California was a long way from New York. They didn't want to be parents, but they desperately wanted to be grandparents. They wanted to be a part of Lucas's life, to watch him grow.

Reed had immediately pledged his jet, his corporate account at a dozen Manhattan hotels, his parents' guest rooms on Long Island, and he offered to send Elizabeth and Lucas to California as often as possible. He explained that he would like nothing better than for the Vances' house to be Lucas's second home when he and Elizabeth needed to be away.

In the end, the Vances had enthusiastically agreed not to contest the will. Reed had wanted to promise a visit for the weekend, but he knew he needed to talk to Elizabeth first.

On the flight home, he grew more and more eager to talk to Elizabeth, and he thought of more and more things he wanted to say.

But, at the airport in New York, he was met by Collin and Selina. They both fell into step with him as he marched toward his limo at the passenger pickup.

"Go away," he told them, determined that for *once* Elizabeth would come first.

"We need to talk to you," said Collin.

"I don't care," said Reed. He was going home, and nothing was going to stop him. He'd pay the damn ten million dollars if that's what it took.

"It's important," said Selina.

"So is my life." Reed pushed open the airport door, coming out onto a floodlit, rain-soaked sidewalk.

"This is about your life," said Collin.

"We have information," said Selina.

"I have a marriage to save," Reed countered, spotting his driver. He marched out from under the awning. The driver rushed forward with an umbrella, relieving Reed of his briefcase.

"We can tell you in the car," Collin offered.

Reed heaved a sigh. "We're going straight to the penthouse. I'm not going to the office, or the police station, and we're not stopping for anything but traffic lights." He looked pointedly at the driver. "And even those are optional."

The man grinned. "Yes, sir."

He glanced back at Selina and Collin who were rapidly developing a drowned rat look.

"Get in," he grumbled.

"It's important," Selina repeated, as they settled into their seats, an apology in her tone.

"It's always important," said Reed. "That's the problem with my life. If I was deciding between Elizabeth and the things that weren't important, I wouldn't have a problem, would I?" He didn't wait for an answer. "But every day, nearly every hour, something that is vitally important grabs my time and attention. I spend my evenings with you two and with Gage and Trent, because if we don't work this out, I might be going to jail. A blackmailer might extort money. Somebody might even die.

"And so I do my part," Reed continued. "But you know what? It stops here. I'm going home to Elizabeth. You two tell me what I need to do to make that happen."

Selina glanced at Collin. "Do you want to tell him or shall I?"

Collin gestured that Selina should go ahead.

"It's the Hammond and Pysanski connection."

"Don't tell me. It's getting worse?" Reed absolutely could not get a break.

"I spent the last two days in Washington," said Selina. "I found out that each of Hammond and Pysanski's purchases were made in the forty-eight hours following the committee's shortlisting of the project in question."

"How many companies on the shortlist?" Reed couldn't help asking. Had Hammond and Pysanski bought into the shortlisted companies on spec?

"Usually three to five," said Selina. "But it looks like the unofficial decision coincided with the shortlist. Because they bought into the right company each and every time."

Reed was dumbfounded. "So, Kendrick is guilty."

"At first I thought it was Kendrick, too. But then I found this." Selina pulled a sheet of paper out of her briefcase. "One of the senator's aides, Clive Neville. With each transaction, the day after the Hammond and Pysanski stock purchase, ten thousand dollars was deposited to Clive Neville's account."

"A payoff?" asked Reed.

Selina nodded. "But you and Gage bought your shares a week before Hammond and Pysanski," she said. "*Before* the shortlist." She smiled at him.

"So it's over?" Reed asked.

Collin slapped him on the shoulder. "It's over."

The limo came to a halt in front of 721 Park Avenue.

Reed handed the bank printout back to Selina. "Well done, team. I hope you don't take this the wrong way. But, goodbye." Reed beat the driver to the door handle and stepped out into the rain.

"You know," said Hanna, topping up their wineglasses with a merlot, "there *is* another option."

"No, there's not." Elizabeth was out of options to save her marriage. All that was left was to save herself. Reed was never going to change. That's why she was taking such drastic action.

Hanna set the empty bottle on the coffee table and leaned back at the opposite end of the sofa. "You could tell him you were wrong, that you love him, and that you want your marriage to work out."

"Yeah," came a deep, male voice, and Elizabeth nearly dropped her wine into her lap. Hanna's eyes went wide, and she twisted toward the penthouse foyer.

"You could do that," said Reed, dropping his keys and sauntering into the room.

"Reed." Hanna swallowed around a dry rasp.

"Hello, Hanna."

"I am *so* sorry," she offered in obvious embarrassment. "I was… We were…"

Reed shook his head. "Don't be sorry. If I thought you'd convince her, I'd leave and let you go at it."

"She won't convince me," said Elizabeth with conviction. It was nearly ten o'clock, and today was just another example of Reed's hectic schedule. He'd flown to Chicago for a meeting. Clearly, he'd spent the entire day there. Just as clearly, he'd had more important things to do than tuck Lucas into bed.

Maybe it was her own fault. Maybe she simply wasn't interesting enough to come home to. Maybe she should have gotten a job years ago and become a more interesting wife for him.

Then again, how would he know whether she was interesting or not? The man wouldn't even show up for a conversation.

Reed picked up the wine bottle, raising his eyebrows when he saw it was empty. "Shall I open another?"

Hanna struggled to get to her feet. "I should really go, and let you two—"

He forestalled her with his palm. "Stay put. You're

obviously on my side. It looks like you two have a head start, but I'd love to joint the party."

Hanna gave Elizabeth a questioning look, which Elizabeth answered with a shrug. It wasn't like she and Reed had any big plans for being alone. In fact, it was probably better to have Hanna here as a foil until bedtime, or at least until Elizabeth got slightly intoxicated.

"Bring on another bottle," she told him.

Reed gave her a genuine smile, and the force of it shot all the way to her toes. She immediately rethought her strategy on getting intoxicated. It could be dangerous to be around him without all her faculties intact. She set her wineglass down on the table.

Reed headed for the wine rack in the dining room.

With him out of the room, Hanna hit Elizabeth with an expression of stark curiosity.

Elizabeth held her palms up in a gesture of confusion. She'd never seen Reed in a mood like this.

He strode back into the living room with an open bottle of wine and three fresh glasses. "The eighty-two Chateau Saint Gaston," he announced with satisfaction.

Elizabeth blinked.

Hanna choked. "Did you just open a ten thousand dollar bottle of wine?"

Reed pretended to study the label. "I do believe I did." He poured them each a glass of the Saint Gaston.

Still standing, he held his glass aloft. "A toast," he said.

"Please don't," begged Elizabeth. She didn't know what he had in mind, but she didn't like the reckless look in his eyes nor the cocky set to his mouth.

"A toast," he said in a softer voice, looking straight into her eyes. "To my gorgeous, gracious, intelligent wife."

"Reed," she pleaded.

"I lied to you today."

So what else was new?

"I wasn't in Chicago."

Something shriveled up inside Elizabeth. The man lied recreationally. She couldn't have cared less whether he was in Chicago.

She waved a dismissive hand. "Whatever. Salute." She lifted her glass to take a drink.

"Uh, uh, uh," he tisked. "This is a ten thousand dollar bottle of wine. Let's have a little respect."

She heaved a frustrated sigh. Maybe she should just go to bed, get to sleep before he decided to join her there. Maybe, just maybe, she'd feel stronger in the morning.

"I was in California," he continued.

Elizabeth waited for the point.

"Ironically, on the advice of my dear father, I went to see the Vances."

She froze. "No." He hadn't compromised their case. He wouldn't.

"And while I was there," he said, "I realized that you, dear Elizabeth, are absolutely right, and I am completely wrong."

He perched himself on the armchair cornerwise to her. "I promise I will never lie to you again."

Elizabeth searched his eyes. They were warm and soft and loving, but she didn't know what to say. "Thank you," she tried.

His lips stretched into a smile before he tipped his glass and took a sip.

Elizabeth followed suit, but she couldn't taste a thing.

"I love you," Reed said to her.

"Hey," Hanna put in, coming to her feet. "I really think I'd better—"

"Drink your wine," Reed ordered. "I might need you later."

She sat back down.

"Where was I?" he asked.

"Are you drunk?" asked Elizabeth, trying desperately to make sense of his behavior. This wasn't the Reed she knew.

"Oh, yes. Now I remember. The Vances are not going to contest the will."

Elizabeth was afraid she hadn't heard that right. "What?"

He nodded his confirmation, slowing down his words. "The Vances are not going after custody of Lucas. And, no, I'm not drunk."

A pulse of optimism hit Elizabeth for the first time in weeks. "How did you…?"

"Skill, intelligence and guile. Plus a really fast private jet."

"Quit messing around," Elizabeth ordered. This was a serious conversation, not a joke.

"Oh, I think I'll mess around a little longer." He took another sip of the wine, holding his glass back to study the legs. "Worth every penny."

"Go, Reed." Hanna applauded in a reverent tone.

"Thank you," said Reed. "Now, will you help me convince her I'm worth sticking with?"

"He's worth sticking with," Hanna said to Elizabeth.

"Traitor," Elizabeth muttered, but even she was running out of excuses to leave him. He might have lied about Chicago, and he might have been gone all day long, but he'd done it for Lucas, and he'd done it for her.

"She told me you were great in bed," Hanna offered.

"Hanna!" Elizabeth was horrified.

"Well, that's one in my column," said Reed.

"Damn straight," said Hanna.

"There's one more thing." He sobered, all traces of joking gone, his attention fixed completely on Elizabeth. "I'll be home evenings from here on in. Or I'll work part-time. Or I'll sell my companies. Or we can move to freakin' Biarritz if that will make a difference."

Elizabeth's throat thickened up. "What are you saying?"

"I'm saying that I'm prepared to put as much effort into my marriage as I put into my business."

Elizabeth was speechless. Her heartbeat sped up and her chest went tight. She stared at Reed in utter astonishment. "Seriously?"

Hanna stuck out her foot and nudged Elizabeth in the knee. "I think the word you're looking for is *yes!*"

Twelve

Elizabeth and Reed were on their way to the bedroom when Lucas stirred. Reed went into the nursery to rock him back to sleep, while Elizabeth all but floated into their bedroom.

Reed was staying. They were going to work things out. He'd decided their love was worth fighting for, and if there was anything her husband could do, it was to achieve whatever goal he set for himself.

Though they'd slept in their bed together hundreds of times, she knew tonight was special. It was the beginning of a whole new marriage, a whole new family.

She pulled open the top drawer of the bureau, and her gaze caught on the rosewood coin box. She slowly lifted the lid, pulling out the liberty head, ten-dollar gold coin, and hefting its weight in her palm.

"Heads," she whispered to herself, "I do it."

Tails, she'd do it anyway. This time, she didn't need to flip the coin.

She slipped it back into its holder and pulled out the red silk negligee she'd worn on her wedding night. Appropriate, since this was another new beginning.

She removed her clothes, but as she was about to slip the soft silk over her head, her gaze caught another flash of fabric in the drawer. Lemon yellow and bright blue and purple. The silk scarves they'd bought in France.

Elizabeth paused. She set the negligee aside, fingering the texture of the scarves. And then she smiled. This wasn't her honeymoon. It was a different beginning, a different relationship, a relationship based on authenticity instead of fantasy.

She wrapped the lemon yellow scarf over her breasts, tying it at the back like a bikini top. Then she fastened the blue and purple one low on her hips, sarong-style, leaving most of one thigh and hip bare. She combed her hair, dabbed some perfume, then waited, standing in the middle of the room.

Reed walked in and stopped, his gaze trailing up and down her body. "We going to Tahiti?" he asked.

She sauntered toward him, walking her fingertips up his chest, snaking her arms around his neck. "I think we're going to nirvana."

A gorgeous smile spread across his face. One arm snaked around to the small of her back, tugging her tight. His other hand cupped her bottom through the soft silk.

"I do love you," he whispered as he bent to kiss her lips.

She tipped her head back, opening her mouth, meeting his hot tongue in a tangle of passion and desire that she couldn't hope to contain. And she wouldn't. It was all honesty all the time from here on in.

She pushed his suit jacket off his shoulders, letting it fall to a heap on the floor. Then she attacked his shirt buttons while he nipped and nibbled his way along her shoulder. His hand slipped under the sarong, toying with her heating skin.

He cupped her breast, strumming his thumb over her hard nipple. "I so love these scarves," he breathed.

"Versatile," she agreed.

He chuckled low, then his tone turned to a growl. "Nobody, nowhere, no how is ever going to stop us from making love. I don't care what the science says, *this* is right."

She nodded her agreement, gasping as his finger slipped inside.

"Too fast?" he asked.

"No. Just right." She grappled with his belt buckle, and he shucked his clothes, pulling her onto the bed in a flurry of caresses, kisses and silk.

When she was naked, he stretched her arms over her head, stroking his fingertips from the wrists all the way to her toes and then back again.

She shuddered at the sensations, freed her hands and caressed the play of his muscles, from his shoulders to his abs and beyond.

He rolled on top of her, settling between her legs, his body teasing her sensitized flesh. He took one nipple into his mouth, drawing out the caress as she squirmed beneath him. Then he laved the other, then moved to her mouth, kissing her long and deeply.

He drew back, gazing down into her eyes as he slowly pushed into her. She felt the pressure, then the heat, then the fullness, and then he stopped. They stared at each other for a frozen moment of perfect communication.

Reed flexed his hips, and sparks shot off in her brain. She tipped her head back, exposing her throat to his kisses. Her hands tangled in his hair, and he murmured her name over and over while time stopped and he drove them higher into the atmosphere, past the moon and the stars, to the outer stratosphere until the entire universe exploded around them.

Elizabeth woke to the sound of Lucas's gurgles and coos in the nursery. Reed's arm was across her stomach, holding her firmly back against his body.

"Good morning, gorgeous," he whispered against her hair.

"Good morning, handsome," she responded.

He planted a series of tender kisses on the back of her neck.

"There's a baby waking up," she warned him, the buzz of desire forming instantly in her belly.

"Can't resist me?" he teased.

"I don't want to resist you," she corrected.

He moaned. "Oh, *that's* what I like to hear."

"But I have to get Lucas."

"I'll get Lucas. You go lounge in the bath for a while."

Elizabeth glanced at the clock. "You'll be late for work."

She felt him shrug. "So, I'll be late for work. Who cares?"

She turned onto her back to stare up at him. "Reed, you don't have to prove—"

"What are they going to do? Fire me?"

"I'm just saying—"

"Bath," he repeated. "What does Lucas eat for breakfast?"

"Oatmeal." She searched his expression. "Are you really…"

"What did you think I meant last night?"

"That you'd get home earlier in the evenings."

"And the rest?"

The part about working part-time or selling his companies or moving to France? "I thought it was a terrific speech."

Some of the light went out of his eyes. "I was serious, Elizabeth."

"Okay." She nodded, realizing he was completely serious. "Okay, husband of mine. Our baby eats oatmeal for breakfast. Sometimes he gets it in his hair. Sometimes he gets it in my hair." She jammed her thumb in the direction of the en suite. "And I'm going to take a very long bubble bath."

"Good for you."

She wrapped her arms around him and held him close, drawing the hug out until Lucas's little voice turned demanding. Then Reed pulled back the covers, and Elizabeth headed for the bathtub.

While the water splashed and foamed its way to the top of the oversize bath, she brushed her teeth, combed her hair, and twisted it into a messy knot on top of her head. She retrieved a soft terry robe from the closet and hung it on the hook on the back of the door.

Rain spattered on the bathroom window, while the small room filled with the scent of roses. Elizabeth took a deep, cleansing breath, glad that the month of October was coming to a close. November was going to be so much better. Maybe they would go to Tahiti.

She slipped a toe into the hot water, then her ankle and calf. The steam caused a sudden wave of vertigo, and she steadied herself on the towel rack. But it passed, and she lowered herself into the luxuriant water.

They'd only had Lucas for three weeks, but already she appreciated the simple pleasure of time for self-indulgence. She pictured Lucas in the high chair, and Reed heating up the oatmeal. She smiled. There would be happy months and years ahead of them.

Months.

Elizabeth blinked.

She sat up, sending a wave of water over the edge of the tub, splashing onto the tile floor.

October was almost over.

Her cycle was off.

Her cycle was way off, and she'd been dizzy getting into the tub, dizzy three days ago in the penthouse foyer. She counted on her fingers.

No way. *No way.* They'd missed her prime ovulating days. They'd gone against all the advice of their doctor.

Yet, still…

Her hands started to shake as she made her way out of the tub. She pulled open the lower cabinet, digging through the bath crystals and shampoo, finally finding an open box containing the second of two pregnancy tests.

She frantically checked the expiration date. She was in under the wire. Then she scanned the instructions, followed them and set the little wand down on the counter, backing away.

From across the room she stared at the little window for three minutes, dripping wet, while the color arranged itself against a white background.

When the time elapsed, she moved forward.

Two lines.

She blinked.

There were *two lines*. She was pregnant. Lucas was going to have a brother or a sister. She and Reed were going to have a baby.

She sat down on the edge of the tub. Her legs were shaking, and a chill came over her body. When the weakness subsided, she wrapped her arms around her abdomen. There was a baby in there. A tiny little baby was growing inside her.

A warm glow enveloped her body.

She stood and wrapped the terry robe around her. Then she tightened the belt and all but floated down the hall to give Reed the good news.

"Iron, calcium, vitamin A, and a good source of fiber," he was reading out loud.

She rounded the corner.

"I kind of like it myself," said Hanna.

Elizabeth stopped short at the sight of Reed, Joe and Hanna surrounding Lucas's high chair.

They all turned to stare at her bulky robe and messy hair.

"Why does this keep happening to me?" she asked.

"Gotta say, babe," Reed said as he gave Elizabeth a kiss on the cheek, "you looked a lot better last time."

Hanna laughed. Even Joe gave a smile.

"Are you on duty?" Elizabeth asked him. If he was going to be hanging around their house, she supposed he'd better get used to her in a bathrobe.

"Just visiting." His hand brushed Hanna's, and Hanna held his fingers for a brief instant.

"Ahh," said Elizabeth.

"I forgot to mention that Selina and Collin solved the SEC problem," said Reed.

Elizabeth spun around to look at him. "It's solved?"

"Yes."

"You're off the hook?"

"It was one of Kendrick's aides. I can give you all the details."

"You're not going to jail?" she confirmed.

Reed nodded.

"And I don't need a bodyguard anymore?"

"Not anymore."

"Those are all the details I need."

Lucas banged his hands on the high-chair tray and chanted a single note.

"So…" She glanced around at the little group. "There's something I need to mention."

They all waited.

"I'm pregnant."

It took a second for her words to sink in.

Hanna squealed and Joe offered congratulations.

Reed simply looked flabbergasted. Then, finally, "How on earth…"

"In Biarritz, I guess," said Elizabeth. It had been scientifically possible, but given her and Reed's history, getting pregnant had seemed highly unlikely.

"Did you do something different?" asked Hanna.

Joe quickly elbowed her.

"That's not what I meant," Hanna protested.

"He tied me to the bedposts," said Elizabeth.

Hanna hooted out a laugh. Joe guffawed.

"I can't believe you said that," Reed told his wife, laughing deep in his throat.

Elizabeth shrugged. "I'm just trying to be honest. And, hey, it worked."

His arms went around her, and he drew her close. "From here on in?" he murmured against her ear. "This honesty thing is just between you and me."

Elizabeth grinned at his words, squeezing him tight as her world settled into a permanent glow of happiness.

* * * * *

Don't miss the next book in
PARK AVENUE SCANDALS,
PREGNANT ON THE UPPER EAST SIDE,
available next month.

*Here's a sneak peek at THE CEO'S CHRISTMAS
PROPOSITION, the first in USA TODAY bestselling
author Merline Lovelace's HOLIDAYS ABROAD
trilogy coming in November 2008.*

American Devon McShay is about to get the
Christmas surprise of a lifetime when she meets
her new client, sexy billionaire Caleb Logan, for
the very first time.

Silhouette
Desire

Available November 2008

Her breath whistled out in a sigh of relief when he exited Customs. Devon recognized him right away from the newspaper and magazine articles her friend and partner Sabrina had looked up during her frantic prep work.

Caleb John Logan, Jr. Thirty-one. Six-two. With jet-black hair, laser-blue eyes and a linebacker's shoulders under his charcoal-gray cashmere overcoat. His jaw-dropping good looks didn't score him any points with Devon. She'd learned the hard way not to trust handsome heartbreakers like Cal Logan.

But he was a client. An important one. And she was willing to give someone who'd served a hitch in the marines before earning a BS from the University of Oregon, an MBA from Stanford and his first million at the ripe old age of twenty-six the benefit of the doubt.

Right up until he spotted the hot-pink pashmina, that is.

Devon knew the flash of color was more visible than the sign she held up with his name on it. So she wasn't surprised when Logan picked her out of the crowd and cut in her direction. She'd just plastered on her best businesswoman smile when he whipped an arm around her waist. The next moment she was sprawled against his cashmere-covered chest.

"Hello, brown eyes."

Swooping down, he covered her mouth with his.

Sheer astonishment kept Devon rooted to the spot for a few seconds while her mind whirled chaotically. Her first thought was that her client had downed a few too many drinks during the long flight. Her second, that he'd mistaken the kind of escort and consulting services her company provided. Her third shoved everything else out of her head.

The man could kiss!

His mouth moved over hers with a skill that ignited sparks at a half dozen flash points throughout her body. Devon hadn't experienced that kind of spontaneous combustion in a while. A *long* while.

The sparks were still popping when she pushed off his chest, only now they fueled a flush of anger.

"Do you always greet women you don't know with a lip-lock, Mr. Logan?"

A smile crinkled the skin at the corners of his eyes. "As a matter of fact, I don't. That was from Don."

"Huh?"

"He said he owed you one from New Year's Eve two years ago and made me promise to deliver it."

She stared up at him in total incomprehension. Logan hooked a brow and attempted to prompt a non-existent memory.

"He abandoned you at the Waldorf. Five minutes before midnight. To deliver twins."

"I don't have a clue who or what you're..."

Understanding burst like a water balloon.

"Wait a sec. Are you talking about Sabrina's old boyfriend? Your buddy, who's now an ob-gyn doc?"

It was Logan's turn to look startled. He recovered faster than Devon had, though. His smile widened into a rueful grin.

"I take it you're not Sabrina Russo."

"No, Mr. Logan, I am *not*."

* * * * *

Be sure to look for
THE CEO'S CHRISTMAS PROPOSITION
by Merline Lovelace.
Available in November 2008
wherever books are sold,
including most bookstores, supermarkets, drugstores
and discount stores.

REQUEST YOUR FREE BOOKS!

2 FREE NOVELS
PLUS 2
FREE GIFTS!

Silhouette®

Desire®

Passionate, Powerful, Provocative!

YES! Please send me 2 FREE Silhouette Desire® novels and my 2 FREE gifts (gifts are worth about $10). After receiving them, if I don't wish to receive any more books, I can return the shipping statement marked "cancel". If I don't cancel, I will receive 6 brand-new novels every month and be billed just $4.05 per book in the U.S. or $4.74 per book in Canada, plus 25¢ shipping and handling per book and applicable taxes, if any*. That's a savings of almost 15% off the cover price! I understand that accepting the 2 free books and gifts places me under no obligation to buy anything. I can always return a shipment and cancel at any time. Even if I never buy another book, the two free books and gifts are mine to keep forever.

225 SDN ERVX 326 SDN ERVM

Name	(PLEASE PRINT)	
Address		Apt. #
City	State/Prov.	Zip/Postal Code

Signature (if under 18, a parent or guardian must sign)

Mail to the Silhouette Reader Service:
IN U.S.A.: P.O. Box 1867, Buffalo, NY 14240-1867
IN CANADA: P.O. Box 609, Fort Erie, Ontario L2A 5X3

Not valid to current subscribers of Silhouette Desire books.

Want to try two free books from another line?
Call 1-800-873-8635 or visit www.morefreebooks.com.

* Terms and prices subject to change without notice. N.Y. residents add applicable sales tax. Canadian residents will be charged applicable provincial taxes and GST. Offer not valid in Quebec. This offer is limited to one order per household. All orders subject to approval. Credit or debit balances in a customer's account(s) may be offset by any other outstanding balance owed by or to the customer. Please allow 4 to 6 weeks for delivery. Offer available while quantities last.

Your Privacy: Silhouette Books is committed to protecting your privacy. Our Privacy Policy is available online at www.eHarlequin.com or upon request from the Reader Service. From time to time we make our lists of customers available to reputable third parties who may have a product or service of interest to you. If you would prefer we not share your name and address, please check here. ☐

SDES08R

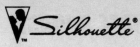

Romantic
SUSPENSE

Sparked by Danger,
Fueled by Passion.

Lindsay McKenna
Susan Grant

Mission: Christmas

Celebrate the holidays with a pair
of military heroines and their daring men
in two romantic, adventurous stories
from these bestselling authors.

Featuring:

"The Christmas Wild Bunch"
by *USA TODAY* bestselling author
Lindsay McKenna
and

"Snowbound with a Prince"
by *New York Times* bestselling author
Susan Grant

Available November wherever books are sold.

COMING NEXT MONTH

#1903 PREGNANT ON THE UPPER EAST SIDE?— Emilie Rose
Park Avenue Scandals
This powerful Manhattan attorney uses a business proposal to seduce his beautiful party planner into bed. After their one night of passion, could she be carrying his baby?

#1904 THE MAGNATE'S TAKEOVER—Mary McBride
Gifts from a Billionaire
When they first met, he didn't tell her he was the enemy. But as they grow ever closer, he risks revealing his true identity and motives, and destroying everything.

#1905 THE CEO'S CHRISTMAS PROPOSITION— Merline Lovelace
Holidays Abroad
Stranded in Austria together at Christmas, it only takes one kiss for him to decide he wants more than just a business relationship. And this CEO always gets what he wants....

#1906 DO NOT DISTURB UNTIL CHRISTMAS— Charlene Sands
Suite Secrets
Reunited with his ex-love, he plans to leave her first this time—until he discovers she's pregnant! Will their marriage of convenience bring him a change of heart?

#1907 SPANIARD'S SEDUCTION—Tessa Radley
The Saxon Brides
A mysterious stranger shows up with a secret and a heart set on revenge. Then he meets the one woman whose love could change all his plans.

#1908 BABY BEQUEST—Robyn Grady
Billionaires and Babies
He proposed a temporary marriage to help her get custody of her orphaned niece, but their passion was all too permanent.

SDCNMBPA1008